What Readers Are Saying about Forbidden Doors

"Nothing I have seen provides better spiritual equipment for today's youth to fight and win the spiritual battle raging around them than Bill Myers's Forbidden Doors series. Every Christian family should have the whole set."

C. Peter Wagner
President, Global Harvest Ministries

"During the past eighteen years as my husband and I have been involved in youth ministry, we have seen a *definite* need for these books. Bill fills the need with comedy, romance, action, and riveting suspense with clear teaching. It's a nonstop page-turner!"

Robin Jones Gunn
Author, Christy Miller series

"There is a tremendous increase of interest by teens in the occult. Everyone is exploiting and capitalizing on this hunger, but no one is providing answers. Until now. I highly recommend the Forbidden Doors series and encourage any family with teens to purchase it."

James Riordan
Music critic and author of the authorized biography of Oliver Stone

"Fast-moving, exciting, and loaded with straightforward answers to tough questions, Forbidden Doors is Bill Myers at his best."

D1053526

The Forbidden Doors Series

The Deceived

BILL MYERS

Tyndale House Publishers, Inc. Wheaton, Illinois

Library of Congress Catalog Card Number 94-60550
ISBN 0-8423-1352-4

Printed in the United States of America

99   98   97   96
9   8   7   6

It is destined that men die only once, and after that comes judgment.

Hebrews 9:27

1

"Where are we going?" Rebecca half croaked, half squeaked. "This isn't the way to the library." She wished her voice was strong and in control, like one of those recording stars. But since this was her first date with Ryan and since her stomach still did little flip-flops every time he smiled at her . . . well, that meant major dry-mouth . . . which meant major no-voice . . . which meant sounding more like Miss Piggy than Whitney Houston.

Ryan broke into another one of his easy grins—the type Becka had fallen for the first day they met. "I have a little friend that wants to meet you," he said. "It'll only take a minute."

Becka tried to swallow, but of course, there was nothing left in her mouth to swallow. She looked out the window of the white Mustang and gave a tug at her tweed skirt. It was shorter than she felt comfortable with—actually any skirt would have been shorter than she felt comfortable with—but Mom thought it looked "adorable." And since wearing sweats probably wasn't the best choice for a first date, there she was, stuck in a skirt, having to do her best imitation of being a lady.

Ryan glanced at the clock on the dashboard. "The guy doesn't start speaking till seven. We've got plenty of time." He turned left off the main road and bounced onto a bumpy side street full of potholes.

Becka wasn't crazy about going to the library to hear the guest speaker. He was one of those New Age fruitcakes who claimed to have been Napoleon or somebody in a past life. The fact that his talk was

sponsored by the Ascension Bookshop
didn't add to her enthusiasm—not since her
little brother's run-in with the Bookshop's
"Society" last week. But that was old news.
Ancient history.

At least she hoped it was.

Unfortunately, Ryan *was* interested in the
guy, Ryan already had tickets, and, most
important, Ryan had asked her to go with
him. So . . . here she was.

She still couldn't figure out why he had
asked her. It certainly wasn't her sparkling
personality. As far as she could tell, anytime
he was around she had none. And it certainly wasn't her looks. Let's face it, being a
five-foot-six bean pole with thin, mousy-
brown hair wouldn't exactly get you in the
swimsuit issue of *Sports Illustrated*. So what
was someone as gorgeous as Ryan doing
with someone as ungorgeous as her?

She continued pondering the question as
she stared out the car window. Outside, the
houses were becoming more and more run-
down. Ryan made another turn and then
another. They followed the street as it
dipped under a low, rusty train trestle and
then rose back up. He slowed the car and
pulled it over to a stop.

The houses were the worst here. They
either needed big-time repairs or a bull-

dozer; Becka wasn't sure which. One thing was certain—they hadn't seen a coat of paint in years. Most of the yards were nothing but dirt with a few clumps of grass here and there that posed as lawns. Half a dozen junk cars were parked in the driveways, in the yards, or beside the curbs—all in various degrees of renovation or dilapidation.

Becka grew uneasy. Poverty was nothing new to her. Growing up in the jungles of Brazil, she'd seen it most of her life. But why had Ryan brought her to this place? What was he up to?

He turned off the car's ignition. "Here we are," he said. Without another word he opened his door and crossed around to her side.

Becka's mind raced. *Is this how it happens? Is this how nice girls wind up on those missing persons posters? They travel to places like this with people they think they can trust, and then . . .* She panicked. *What should I do!?* She glanced to the door locks. *I could lock them. I could lock them, hop behind the wheel, take off, and leave Ryan in the dust to walk home. Yes!*

Her hand started toward the lock, then paused. *What if I'm wrong? I'll be the laughingstock of the school. . . . But which is worse? Being the laughingstock of school or guest starring on the side of some milk carton?*

4

She watched as Ryan approached, brushing the jet-black hair out of his eyes and breaking into another grin. Becka's stomach flipped again and she shook her head. She could trust Ryan McPherson. She knew it.

"Where are we?" she asked as he opened her door.

"Definitely on the wrong side of the tracks." His deep blue eyes sparkled as he held out his hand to help her from the car. Becka could easily get out on her own, but the guy was sweet to offer, so she took his hand and let him help.

The sun had already set, leaving just a few bands of red and violet across the horizon. As usual for this time of year, the fog was billowing in from the beach. Becka pulled her jacket closer and folded her arms to hold back the chill.

"Hey, McPherson! You're late!"

They turned to see a skinny kid, nine or ten years old, scamper down the grade of the train tracks behind them.

"Pepe," Ryan called, "what's up?"

The kid wore a dirty T-shirt, torn pants, and no socks.

Immediately Becka's heart went out to him. How could she have been so stupid? Poverty didn't mean people were bad. It meant they were struggling to keep up, strug-

gling against hunger, ignorance, disease—
the very things her folks had fought against
in South America . . . before her dad died.

Once again she looked over the neighbor-
hood—at the sagging houses, the ragged
kids playing in a vacant lot—and this time
she saw them for what they were: people.
Like herself. But in need.

As Pepe arrived and high-fived Ryan, he
gave Becka the once-over. *"¡Qué bien!"* he
said with a mischievous grin, winking at
Ryan.

Ryan laughed. "English, my man. Talk
English."

Pepe turned to Becka. "I said the pretty
lady is almost as beautiful as what he's been
bragging about."

Rebecca felt her ears grow hot from the
compliment. She threw a glance to Ryan. He
seemed as calm and unflustered as ever.

"How's your mom?" Ryan asked.

Pepe shrugged.

"No change?"

Another shrug. "The doctors, they say if
she doesn't keep taking her medicine, she'll
get a sickness they can't cure."

Ryan frowned. "You tell your mom the
doctor's right. TB's a tricky thing. Even if
she thinks she's getting better, she still has to
keep taking the medicine."

6

Pepe shrugged again. Then, turning to Becka, he grinned. "So, the pretty lady's come to see the Death Bridge?" he asked, motioning to the train trestle behind them.

"Death Bridge?" Becka asked.

Pepe turned to Ryan. "You didn't tell her about our Death Bridge? Doesn't she want to see it?"

"Next time," Ryan said. "We need to get going."

Pepe gave another mischievous grin. "Got other plans, huh?"

Ryan tousled the boy's hair. "Not what you're thinking, amigo."

Becka looked to the ground as her ears grew hotter.

"Listen," Ryan continued, "you'd better be heading home. Your momma's probably worried." He turned back to the car to open the door for Becka, but Pepe quickly stepped in and beat him to it.

"It was a pleasure finally meeting you," he said as he held open the door.

"Thanks," Rebecca said, smiling. She stepped inside, but Pepe did not shut the door. Instead, he hung on it and continued talking. "I've heard soooo much about you." He flashed another smile.

The heat from Becka's ears spread to her face.

"Pepe," Ryan scolded as he crossed to his own side of the car.

Pepe shrugged and pushed her door shut, but he kept right on smiling.

Ryan climbed in and fired up the car. Becka reached for the seat belt. Fastening it would give her something to do to cover her embarrassment. "Cute kid," she heard herself say. "How'd you two meet?"

"I'm in the Big Brother program," Ryan answered as he pulled the car onto the road and made a U-turn. "He doesn't have a dad, so I come down a couple of times a week, you know, just to hang out."

Becka's heart swelled. Imagine a high school guy taking time from his busy schedule to help someone like Pepe. She stole another look in Ryan's direction. What other secrets lay behind that heartbreaker grin of his?

They passed Pepe and gave a final wave. The boy returned it and shouted, *"¡Salud, amor, y mucha familia!"*

"What'd he say?" Becka asked.

Ryan gave a self-conscious smile. "Nothing."

"No," Becka insisted. She was pleased to see that Ryan could also be embarrassed. "What did he say?"

Ryan pushed the hair out of his eyes.

"Tell me," she prodded.

"He wished us health, love . . . and many children."

Rebecca giggled. It was either that or die of embarrassment. Ryan laughed, too, and she liked that. In fact, she was liking everything about this guy.

As they approached the train trestle, she looked up at the brown, rusting girders. The tracks were about twenty feet above. "Why do they call this the Death Bridge?" she asked.

Ryan gave no answer.

Still smiling, she turned to him, but his grin was already gone. "Ryan?" she repeated. "Why do they call this the Death Bridge?"

They were directly under the trestle when Ryan finally answered. There was no humor in his voice. Not even a trace of a smile. "Every year . . . one or two kids . . . they die up there."

~

"BEAM ME UP, SCOTTY, BEAM ME UP!"

"Not now," Scott muttered as he remained hunched over the open encyclopedia. He had the same brown hair and thin frame as his "big" sister, Rebecca. Fortunately his arms were starting to thicken and his shoulders were starting to widen. That, along with

his cracking voice, were sure signs of man-
hood sneaking up just around the corner.
But as far as Scott was concerned, it was
sneaking way too slowly.

At the moment he was reading a section on
rain forest butterflies—but for all he knew it
could have been on Barney the Dinosaur. His
eyes had quit focusing quite a while back. Now
he just hoped that by staring at the words, the
information would somehow sink in.

"BEAM ME UP, BEAM ME UP! *SQUAWK!*
BEAM ME UP!"

"Cornelius, I said not—"

Suddenly his face was full of green and
red feathers. One thing you could say about
the family parrot, he never took no for an
answer. Another thing you could say is that
he hated being ignored. The bird began
prancing back and forth across the pages of
the book, bobbing his head up and down,
making it impossible for Scott to read.

Scott let out a heavy sigh, reached for his
pencil, and began scratching under Cornelius's chin with the eraser. The bird
scrunched and craned his neck until the
pencil hit the perfect spot.

It was quarter to eight. Darryl would be
there any minute to help work on their rain
forest report. And since Scott still had nothing prepared, and since he was still clueless

about their topic, he did the only thing he
could do . . . he closed the book, snapped
on his computer, and dialed up the local bulletin board. It was time for another break.

He typed in his password. A moment later
the words appeared on his screen:

Hello, New Kid, you have a message. Read Now?
Y OR N

"New Kid" was his handle, the name he
used on the bulletin board. He rolled his
mouse over to *Y* and clicked it. More words
appeared.

To: New Kid
From: Z

Scott's interest stirred. Of all the people
on the bulletin board, Z was the greatest
mystery. He never revealed information
about himself, but he always seemed to
know what was going on—especially when
it came to stuff about the occult and the
supernatural. In fact, if it hadn't been for
Z's help last week, Scott could have been
seriously hurt by his "little encounter" with
the Society.

He paged down the screen and read the
message:

It has been several days since we last spoke.
Have you had any more problems with the
Society? If you wish to talk, I will be back on-line
around 9:00. Say hello to Rebecca for me.
Z

A chill swept across Scott's shoulders. He
had never told Z he had a sister. And he had
never mentioned her name.

~

Becka and Ryan were a few minutes late
when they entered the auditorium and took
their seats toward the back. The lecture had
already started, but Becka barely noticed.
Her mind was still on the conversation she
and Ryan had had back at the train trestle.

"You mean they just stand up on that
bridge and wait for the train to come?" she
had asked.

"It's a courage thing," Ryan had
explained. "A power trip. They wait in the
middle till the train comes, then they race it
back to the end of the bridge and jump out
of the way."

"And the last one to jump . . . ?"

"Wins," Ryan had answered. "Unless he
doesn't jump fast enough. Then he loses.
Big-time."

Rebecca shuddered. Even here, in the

warmth of the auditorium, the thought gave her the creeps. She wanted to ask more, but she knew she'd have to wait until after the lecture.

She turned her attention to the speaker. Maxwell Hunter was good-looking with a tan face, a distinguished beard, thick silver hair, and an expensive suit. But what really caught Becka's attention were his eyes. They didn't just scan back and forth across the audience; they seemed to probe people, locking onto them, connecting with each of them as if they really mattered.

"You see," he was saying, "reincarnation is the perfect answer to the age old question, If there's a loving God, why is there suffering?" He paused to take a drink of water, then continued. Once again his eyes swept the room, looking at members of the audience. "Stop and think about it. Is it fair that some people are mentally retarded and others are geniuses? Is it fair that some are physically handicapped and others are Olympic athletes? Is it fair that some starve to death in garbage dumps and others live in palaces? Of course not."

At last Maxwell's eyes connected with Becka's. The effect was startling—as though he had peered into her soul. It only lasted a second, but she was certain he had learned something about her. And then he was gone, peering into someone else.

"Life is completely unfair, unless—" he lowered his voice and continued with quiet intensity— "unless people are suffering now for the evil they have performed in the past . . . unless people are rewarded in this life for the good they've performed in past lives. You see, if we truly believe in a loving God, a compassionate 'Force,' then reincarnation is certainly a viable possibility."

Becka had never given much thought to reincarnation. As far as she figured, it was just another one of those weird Eastern religions where people were afraid to kill a cow because it might wind up being their great-grandmother or something. But Maxwell's idea was intriguing. Reincarnation, the way he described it, *would* explain why some people suffer and others have it so good. Becka frowned and bit her lip. That idea sure beat the thought that God was up there playing games with people's lives and destinies.

"But don't just take my word for it," he continued. "Reincarnation can be proven. That's right. It can be proven absolutely and scientifically."

Becka leaned forward. The man definitely had her attention.

Maxwell stepped down from the stage and walked into the audience as he went on. "Every day thousands of people are remembering their past lives—either on their own or through hypnotic regression." He looked at the audience. "People like you and me. People who recall historical times, dates, facts . . . down to the tiniest detail. Not because they read about them, but because they lived them. Some people can even speak in foreign languages. Not because they've learned them in the here and now, but because they spoke them in the past."

He paused to let his words sink in. There was a shuffling of feet and some quiet murmurings. After a moment, he resumed. "These just aren't folks with overactive imaginations. These are people who seem to have firsthand experience with things they have never seen, who know things they have never learned—impressions, events, foreign languages—all verified by historians as 100 percent accurate!"

The murmuring increased.

Maxwell smiled. "But, as I said, don't take my word for it. Let's find out for ourselves." He stopped and carefully looked over the audience. "May I have some volunteers? Are there a dozen or so people courageous enough to go up on that stage and let me prove my point?"

A few hands shot up immediately. Becka glanced around and wondered how many of the willing volunteers belonged to the Society. Other hands rose a little more tentatively.

Maxwell started to move through the room, nodding and pointing. "You sir, yes you . . . and you ma'am. Just go up on the stage and have a seat. I'll be there in a minute." He continued through the crowd. "And you . . . and you . . ."

Others started to rise and move toward the stage.

"And you . . ." He drifted in Becka's and Scott's direction. "And you ma'am . . . yes, and you." He paused to scan the room. "I still need half a dozen more."

A few other hands slowly rose. He continued moving toward the back of the room. "And you sir . . . and you . . ."

Now he was less than ten feet away from Becka. "And you, yes . . ." His eyes scanned across Becka, then he nodded to Ryan. "And you son."

Becka looked to Ryan with a start, surprised to see his hand raised.

"And your friend, too."

Becka spun back to the man. "Me?" But he'd already moved past them and across

the aisle. Ryan rose to his feet, taking
Becka's hand. She held back.

Ryan smiled down at her and gave a little
tug. "Come on," he whispered. "It should be
fun."

Rebecca shook her head. Being on stage
in front of everyone was not her idea of fun.
But Ryan kept insisting.

"Come on," he coaxed.

A few looked in their direction, and Becka
could feel her ears start to burn. Ryan
flashed her another one of his smiles. She
felt herself weakening. Other people turned
in their direction to check out the commo-
tion. By the look in Ryan's eyes, Becka could
tell he wasn't going to take no for an answer.
She realized she'd be making more of a
scene by staying than by following.

Ryan gave another tug on her hand, his
smile breaking into a grin.

Reluctantly, Becka allowed herself to be
pulled from the seat. They headed down to
the platform, hand in hand.

"Don't worry," Ryan whispered as they
stepped up onto the platform. "I won't let
anything happen to you."

Becka wished he was right. Unfortunately,
wishes don't always come true. . . .

2

Becka continued
to fall . . . backwards . . . slowly . . . softly . . .
as in a dream—gently drifting, lower and
lower. At first the sensation frightened her,
but soon she gave in to it. Soon she was feeling a strange and wonderful sense of detachment and a peace that said everything would
work out—that someone or something far
greater than she was taking control.

19

"That's it," Maxwell's voice continued to soothe, "concentrate on your breathing . . . just your breathing. In . . . and out . . . in . . . and out . . . ."

With her eyes closed, everything around Becka was cotton-soft, velvety-still. She had no idea how long she had been sitting on the stage. She no longer cared. Earlier, she'd felt the sweaty palms and the embarrassment of everyone staring. Out of pure desperation she had focused on Maxwell's voice, his softly spoken commands. And now, as she concentrated on her breathing, as she kept her eyes closed and remained focused, she no longer cared about the audience. She no longer cared about anything, except—

The falling. The gentle, peaceful falling.

Suddenly she was six years old again, floating on her back in a lake. She even recognized the lake. It was one she'd gone swimming in when she was a kid. She could feel the water lapping in her ears, closing around her face, but never quite reaching her mouth. She knew as long as she stayed relaxed, as long as she concentrated on her breathing, she would stay afloat.

Maxwell's voice echoed around her, soft and calming. "Listen to your breath; it is your life force. . . . Keep emptying your

mind . . . letting go . . . drifting backward. . . ."

The lake around Becka slowly dissolved.
The water became layers of color. Soft reds,
burgundies, purples. She was falling again,
but now she was falling through the layers of
color. One after another. But they weren't
just layers of color. They were layers of emotions . . . and memories.

A tender face looked down at her through
the colors. *Daddy!* Sudden feelings choked
Becka. How she missed him! Six months had
passed since he had died, and she still ached
to be with him, to hear his voice, to feel him
holding her. It was an ache she knew would
never leave—a pain deep inside, that no one
could ever remove.

And yet—there he was, looking at her,
his face gentle and loving. He was younger
than she remembered, except from photo-
graphs. He still had his beard—the one
Mom had made him shave off after Scotty
was born. She could feel his big hands
wrap around her as he scooped her into
his arms.

He began to sing. At first she couldn't
hear the words, but the voice grew louder.
They were lyrics she had forgotten—lyrics
from long ago. As she listened, a tight knot
of emotion formed in the back of her throat.

Ride a little horsey, to town, to town,
Ride a little horsey, to town, to town,
Careful, Becky, don't fall . . . down.

With the last word, he pretended to drop her just a few inches. She heard herself gurgle in delight. How she loved the feel of those hands wrapped around her, holding her. She wanted to touch him, to reach out and stroke his beard. But as her hand rose, his face faded.

Again she was falling backward.

Soon she was someplace even warmer, even more secure—surrounded by soft reds and pinks . . . and lots of warm, soothing liquid. She looked at her hands—and her eyes widened in surprise: They were the hands of an unborn baby! She'd seen pictures of babies in the womb in science class, and their hands were just like this, pink and translucent. The fingers were nearly formed, but not quite.

I'm—I'm not even born yet! I'm still inside Mom! she thought. *This is too weird!* But Becka wasn't afraid. In fact, she had never felt so protected. So tranquil.

And still she fell. Farther and farther back . . .

Then she heard voices, faint at first, but growing louder. Harsh voices. Mocking voices. She tried to make out the words, but they were gibberish.

She tried to move, to see who was there, but she was suddenly struck in the back, and she fell to her knees. Momentarily stunned, she struggled to catch her breath and slowly realized she was kneeling on a bloody, wooden platform.

It was night. The voices were much louder now. Glancing cautiously around, Becka saw people carrying torches and dressed in clothes she had only seen in movies and history books. They shoved and pushed at each other, trying to break past the guards who surrounded the platform. Becka stared in confusion at the guards' weapons: ancient rifles and bayonets. The people shouted, they screamed, they jeered. Suddenly it struck her: They were shouting and screaming and jeering at her!

She tried again to lift her head and was struck again. She tried to move her hands, but they were tied behind her back.

Where am I?

Suddenly hands grabbed her by the hair, dragging her onto a small table, forcing her onto her stomach, and shoving her head down onto a bloody wooden block.

To her right she could just see a wooden pillar. Beyond that and below was the screaming mob. She looked to the left. Another wooden pillar. And beside that a fat, muscular man. She looked to his face and gasped. He wore a black hood with two holes cut out for eyes.

"Where am I?" she cried. "What's going on?!"

He paid no attention.

Somewhere, a group of drums began to roll and then stop. They rolled again, then stopped. They started a third time. Only now they did not stop but kept rolling and rolling and rolling. The crowd yelled louder, working themselves into a frenzy.

Becka squirmed and strained. With great effort she turned her head to follow one of the wooden pillars as it reached skyward. And then she saw it. A giant blade—ten, maybe fifteen feet above her head. Its sharpened edge glistened in the light of the torches.

A guillotine! she thought. *I'm in a guillotine!*

The drums continued to roll. Becka turned back to the hooded man. He was holding the rope taut, keeping the blade suspended above her.

"No!" she cried. "It's a mistake! NO!"

She twisted her head back up to the steel blade just as the man released the rope. The blade fell, plummeting toward her.

"NOOOO . . . !"

~

"Miss, come out of it. You're back with us, now. . . . Miss . . . Miss . . ."

Someone was shaking her.

"Becka, it's OK! I'm here. I'm here. . . ."

Her eyes fluttered, then opened. She was back on the stage in the library—covered in sweat and gasping for breath.

"It's OK," Ryan repeated. He had dropped to his knees and was holding her. "Becka, I'm here, it's OK, it's OK. . . ."

She clung to him fiercely. Her eyes darted wildly to the audience staring up at her.

"It's OK, it's OK. . . ."

She continued fighting for breath, her chest heaving. But she was safe. She was back home. She was in Ryan's arms.

~

"And you're sure this Z fellow is a good guy?" Darryl asked, his voice high and squeaky. Scott grimaced. As the "all-school dweeb," Darryl's voice was supposed to squeak. It was expected. Just like it was expected that he would be half a foot shorter than anybody else, dress in last year's hand-me-downs, and have a haircut that . . . well, let's just say if the Beatles ever came back, he'd be right in style.

For some reason the little guy had picked Scott out as his best friend. Of course Scott had tried to get out of the deal, but he was just too nice. Besides, as the new kid in town, Scott really couldn't be that picky. He'd take whatever friends he could get.

Darryl plopped onto Scott's bed and bit into one of the apples they'd just scored from the downstairs fridge. Like Scott, he knew they had to prepare a major report on the rain forest. And, like Scott, he knew it was the last thing in the world he wanted to do. That was OK, though. With any luck, they could stretch this Z mystery out all night so they'd never have to crack a book.

Scott answered Darryl's question. "As far as I can tell, he's OK. I mean, he sure helped me out with the Society and all that Ouija board junk."

Darryl took another bite of apple. "And you're positive you never talked to him about your sister?"

Scott nodded and motioned toward the computer. "I save all the messages. I went through them before you got here."

"And?"

"I never mentioned Becky—not once."

Darryl toyed with the stem of his apple,

thinking. "I have this computer-hacker friend—well, actually he's a cousin—anyway, he claims he can get into any computer system and get any information."

"What's that got to do with me?" Scott asked. He glanced at the radio alarm on his nightstand. It had just flipped to 8:58. In a couple of minutes Z would be back on-line.

Darryl gave a loud sniff. (Besides a squeaky voice, he was always giving his nose a workout—sniffing and snorting and sometimes spitting. It drove Scott crazy, but outside of slipping a cold capsule into the kid's drink every twelve hours, there wasn't much he could do.) "It means," Darryl said, sniffing again, "if you really want to find out who this Z guy is, my cousin can break into the bulletin board system, trace Z's line, and get his address."

"He can do that?" Scott asked.

"No sweat."

Scott started gnawing on his left thumbnail. He always chewed his nails when he thought. Finally he shook his head. "Nah, that would be too mean. The guy obviously wants his privacy."

Darryl pushed up his glasses and gave another sniff. Scott snapped on the computer and dialed up the bulletin board.

With a few keystrokes and a click or two of the mouse, he was on-line and typing:

> *Z, are you there? This is New Kid.*
> *Z?*

After a moment the words finally formed on the screen:

> Hello, New Kid.

"It's him," Scott half-whispered.

Darryl sat up on the bed and watched as more words formed. It was odd seeing letters appear on the computer screen with no one typing on the keyboard. But that's how it worked. All the information moved back and forth through the phone line.

> How are you and your sister adjusting to our city?

Scott exchanged glances with Darryl. Then, with a deep breath, he typed:

> *How do you know about my sister?*

There was no answer. Scott waited tensely. Still nothing. Finally he typed:

> *Are you there? Z?*

The pause continued. Then letters slowly appeared:

There are some things you must not know. In
time, perhaps, but not now.

Scott and Darryl looked at each other. But Z wasn't finished.

How is Rebecca?
Are you changing the subject?
Yes.

"Well," Scott sighed, "at least the guy's honest." He leaned back over the keyboard.

*Becka's at a lecture at the library. Some New Age
hypnotist guy.*
Z?
Tell her to be careful.
Why?
Hypnotism can be tricky.

Scott gave a snort.

Are you telling me hypnotism isn't good?

Another pause, another answer.

Opinion is divided. Some feel hypnotism is helpful

29

for patients in clinical situations. Others feel the hypnotic trance is the exact state that mediums and witches have been using for thousands of years to communicate with spirits.

Scott and Darryl stared at the screen. Scott typed:

> How do you know all this stuff?
> Z?

Finally the words appeared:

> I know.
> But how? How do you know?
> Good night, New Kid.
> Z. Don't go. Wait a minute! Z!

But Z had signed off. Scott angrily disconnected the line and shut off the computer.

There was a long moment of silence. Darryl sniffed. More silence. Than a louder snort. Finally Darryl asked the question running through both of their minds. "So you really think you can trust him?"

Scott turned to look at his friend.

"Just say the word," Darryl said with a shrug. "We can find out who he is and he'll never know. Just say the word."

Scott took a deep breath and slowly let it

out. "OK," he finally said. "As long as he won't know."

~

Rebecca's head ached.

"Are you certain you're all right?" Maxwell asked.

She rubbed the back of her neck. "Yes," she answered for the hundredth time. "I'm OK."

By now most of the crowd had left. There were still a few hangers-on scattered around the stage—mostly the weirdo fringe who wanted to talk to Maxwell about weirdo fringe stuff. But he showed no interest in them. All of his attention was focused on Becka and Ryan.

"That was one of the most intense experiences I've ever witnessed," he said as he walked with them toward the side exit. "Especially for a first timer. Are you certain you've never practiced hypnotic regression before?"

"Not in this lifetime." Becka tried to laugh at her little joke. It only made her head throb worse.

Maxwell smiled. He turned to Ryan. "Take her straight home."

Ryan nodded.

Turning back to Becka, Maxwell continued, "You'll need plenty of rest. Take some

31

aspirin. Oh, and chamomile tea; that is
always good. It will help you relax."

Becka nodded. "Thanks."

They arrived at the door.

"Rebecca . . ."

It was the first time the man had used her
name. It was just as startling and unnerving
as the first time his eyes had connected with
hers. She hesitated, then looked up to meet
his eyes. Once again she felt him entering
her soul, uncovering her thoughts. He held
the gaze a long moment before finally speaking. "There is a greatness about you. You
don't fully understand your power yet, but if
you listen to your past, if you let the power
emerge, it will unlock remarkable talents
within you."

Becka swallowed and continued staring.
She wasn't sure she could look away, even if
she wanted to.

"Would it be possible. . . ." He chose his
words carefully. "Would you mind if I visited
you and your parents sometime this week?"

Becka's eyes widened in surprise.

Immediately, Maxwell apologized. "I am
sorry. After all you have been through . . .
that was terribly insensitive. I do apologize."
He reached into his suit pocket and pulled
out a business card. "I will be in town for five
more days." He began writing a phone num-

ber on the back. "If for any reason you wish to talk with me about your experience or if you have any questions, please call this number."

He handed her the card. She looked down at it a long moment.

"Becka?"

Rebecca looked up. Ryan held open the door for her, waiting for her to pass.

"Thanks," she mumbled as she stepped into the foggy night of the parking lot.

"It was a pleasure meeting you," Ryan called over his shoulder.

"Yes," Becka said, remembering her manners. "It was a—"

"No, Rebecca," Maxwell spoke with such authority that both Becka and Ryan stopped and turned. Maxwell remained at the door, smiling broadly. "The pleasure was mine."

3

The following
morning Rebecca stumbled to the breakfast
table half asleep. She hadn't told Scott what
had happened in the library auditorium.
Somehow, she knew he wouldn't approve—
especially after his little run-in with the Society the week before. And if she hadn't told
him about being hypnotized, she definitely
wasn't going to tell him about her dreams.

35

The dreams. Talk about weird. All night they'd come at her: screaming mobs, guillotines, little Pepe, the Death Bridge—and a few dozen thundering trains thrown in just to keep things lively. Everything was jumbled together. Nothing made sense. But that didn't stop them from coming again and again . . . and again. By morning Becka was more exhausted than when she'd gone to bed.

Mom flitted about the kitchen, eating dry toast and asking if her sleeveless dress made her look too heavy for her upcoming job interview. Of course, she also wanted to know every detail of Becka's date.

Unfortunately, the word *fine* was about all she could get out of Becka that morning.

"How was your date?"

"Fine."

"How was the lecture?"

"Fine."

"How was Ryan?"

"Fine."

Usually the two shared everything. Clothes, shoes, girl talk. They had always been close, and now that Dad was gone, they were even closer . . . when they weren't fighting about the usual mom/daughter stuff. Becka knew her mom wasn't happy with her answers, but for this morning, "fine" would have to do—at least till Scott wasn't around.

Becka and Scott were also good friends
. . . when they weren't fighting about the
usual brother/sister stuff. But there was
something about her experience at the
library that she knew he wouldn't like. And
she definitely wasn't in the mood for an
argument—not this morning.

At the moment Scott was plowing through
his second or third bowl of Kix and chatter-
ing on about uncovering Z's true identity.
Becka pretended to listen, but she barely
heard. Her mind still churned over her experience at the library. And over her dreams.

What had Maxwell said? *"There is greatness
about you. Listen to your past. . . . Let your powers emerge?"*

What kind of greatness? What kind of powers? Becka sighed. The guy was probably just
making it all up. But the image of the guillotine suddenly flashed through her mind.
That had certainly been real enough. And
what about those crazy dreams?

Maybe there's something to all this after all. . . .

~

Forty-five minutes later Becka entered Crescent Bay High. As far as schools go, it was
pretty cool. Unfortunately that was her problem. The school was cool, but she wasn't.
Something about growing up in the jungles

of Brazil keeps you a little out of touch with the latest California fashions and trends. But through trial and error (mostly error), she was learning.

Becka had barely entered the hallway when Julie Mitchell joined her. As usual, Julie wore the perfect clothes—loose shorts, a too-cool sweatshirt, killer shoes—all coordinated to look perfectly casual while, at the same time, calculated to show off her perfect body and her perfect, thick, blonde hair. Normally Becka totally avoided spoiled rich kids. But Julie was different. She didn't have the ego or the attitude. She was downright nice. She'd been friendly to Becka the first day they met. And as they worked out together in track and hung out together at lunch, their friendship grew.

"So how's Super Celeb?" Julie asked as they headed down the hall.

"Super what?"

"Hey, Becka, how's it going?" a voice called.

Rebecca looked over to see a couple of jocks in letterman jackets. They leaned against the lockers, grinning. She wasn't sure which one had spoken, but it didn't matter. Twenty-four hours ago neither of them had known she existed. She glanced down to make sure she hadn't put her pants on backwards or made some other tactical mistake in wardrobe. Nope, as far as she could tell, everything was normal—just your basic, average clothes on your basic, ho-hum body.

Others kids passed, also smiling, also nodding.

"Hey, Beck."

"How's it going, Becka?"

She looked to Julie and whispered, "What's going on?"

"Everybody's talking about last night. I guess you put on quite a show."

"Tell me about it," she muttered, feeling her face start to flush.

"Don't be so gloomy." Julie chuckled. "Everyone thinks it's cool. They say Maxwell spent all sorts of time with you afterward. Even gave you his phone number."

"Hello, Becka." A couple of freshmen girls passed and giggled, obviously showing off for the others around them.

"So, when you calling him?" Julie lowered her voice, pretending to sound ominous. "When's he going to tell you your mysterious past?"

Rebecca took a deep breath. All morning she had been struggling with that same question. What she had experienced up on the stage was real; there was no doubt about it. But remembering it still gave her the creeps.

"I don't know," she sighed. "I mean, he seemed nice and everything, but—"

"But what?" Julie prodded.

"Isn't he friends with the kids in the Society and with the Ascension Lady from the Bookshop? I mean, didn't she, like, sponsor his talk?"

"So?" Julie asked. "Look, I know she messed me up with those charms and stuff, but that doesn't mean everything she does is bad."

Becka took another breath.

Julie continued. "You're the one that had the vision or whatever it was. You're the one who's supposed to have all of this untapped power. Not the Ascension Lady and not that Maxwell guy. It's you. And if you ask me, you'd be pretty stupid not to at least check it out."

They arrived at Julie's locker, and she dialed up her combination.

"Hey, Rebecca." A couple of senior guys approached. Cute. Very cute. They nodded and ambled past without another word.

Julie and Becka turned to watch. Yes, very cute indeed. "Go for it," Julie giggled. "What do you have to lose?"

Julie was right. What did she have to lose? It was just your basic hypnotism, the same stuff doctors and psychiatrists used every day. And Julie was right about another thing. If she *had* been someone great in a previous life, if she *did* hold some kind of secret powers, wasn't it her responsibility to find out?

By two-thirty Rebecca had made up her mind. It wasn't just the attention she received—although being looked upon as someone with super, hidden powers didn't hurt. And it wasn't just the expectations Julie, Ryan, Krissi, and the other kids at the lunch table seemed to have of her. It was also the expectations she had of herself. All of her life she had lived in the background. Scotty was the star of the family; she was the "nonperson," the nobody no one ever noticed. But now . . . now she had a chance to be a somebody everybody would notice. Didn't she owe it to herself to at least find out?

All it would take was one little phone call.

With Ryan at her side, Becka headed for the pay phone near the office. But as she approached she found herself slowing.

"Go ahead," Ryan urged. "It's just a call." Rebecca looked at him. He gave her another one of his heartbreaker smiles. "I'm right here. . . . What can happen?"

He was right, of course. It was just a call. And with him at her side, what could happen?

With a nervous smile she lifted the

receiver, dropped in the coins, and dialed the number on the back of Maxwell Hunter's business card.

~

Scott stood beside Darryl as the kid knocked on the blistered and peeling front door. But it wasn't just the front door that was blistered and peeling—the whole house was that way. Then there were the added attractions of broken shutters, a crumbling chimney, and a rotting porch. The place looked like it belonged in some sort of horror flick.

"You sure Gomez and Morticia are expecting us?" Scott quipped, trying to fight off the jitters.

"Don't be fooled," Darryl squeaked. "On the outside Hubert is a slob, but on the inside he's a genius."

A voice barked through the intercom near the door. "Who is it?"

Darryl tilted his head toward a surveillance camera mounted on the porch roof.

"It's me. Darryl." He pushed up his glasses and gave a sniff.

"What do you want?" the voice demanded.

"I brought a friend. We need your help."

"Not interested! Go away."

"See," Darryl said as he turned to Scott. "I told you he couldn't help us."

42

Before Scott could respond, the voice interrupted. "What's that?"

Darryl gave Scott a wink and turned back to the camera. "I told my friend our problem was too hard for you, that you'd never be able to solve it."

"Says who?"

Darryl just shrugged.

"Why'd you come here if you didn't think I could solve it?"

"My mistake," Darryl said as he turned to leave.

"Hold it. Wait a minute."

"No, you're right." Darryl started down the steps. "We'll find somebody else."

"Hold it, I said!" The voice paused. "All right, come on up—but just for a minute."

Darryl grinned slyly as the door buzzed and they pushed it open. "It works every time," he whispered.

The first thing Scott noticed when he entered was the smell. It was like a giant cat box that hadn't been emptied in weeks. Make that months. Then he saw the reason. Cats. Dozens of them, lying on the floor, curled up on dusty furniture, and spread out on the stairway that lay in front of them.

"Come on." Darryl headed for the stairs and motioned for Scott to follow. "Just don't step on the cats. He's kind of partial to them."

"I noticed."

They made their way up the stairs, threading around the cats, ducking the cobwebs, and sidestepping more Domino's Pizza boxes than Scott could count.

"He likes pizza too." Darryl explained.

Upstairs was just as cluttered. Electrical parts were scattered everywhere—radio chassis, TV cabinets, circuit boards, coils of copper wire, radios, speakers, giant insulators from power lines. The place looked like a Radio Shack gone berserk.

"Over here," a voice called from a room to the right. They turned to see a skinny guy with no shirt. He was hunched over a table piled high with gutted printers, computers, telephones, modems, and whatnots. The guy's hair was frizzy, his face unshaven, and his glasses were held together with masking tape. At the moment he was soldering a circuit board with one hand and wiping his nose with the back of the other.

"Scott—" Darryl beamed as they approached the room and entered— "I want you to meet my cousin Hubert."

Both Darryl and Hubert sniffed in perfect unison. Somehow Scott wasn't surprised they were related.

Hubert never looked up. He stayed hunched over the table, soldering. "So what's this unsolvable problem?" he asked.

"We gotta get the address of somebody who's talking with Scott on a local bulletin board."

"Which one?" Hubert sniffed.

"Uh . . . it's called Night Light," Scott answered.

"No problem." Hubert sniffed.

Darryl grinned. "I told you."

"But . . ." Scott took a hesitant step closer. "We don't want him to know we know. He kinda likes his privacy."

"No problem." Hubert repeated. He pushed up his glasses and continued soldering.

The two boys stood in silence. Scott cleared his throat. "So, uh, how're you going to do it?"

"Simple," was the answer.

More silence. More fidgeting. Another question from Scott. "How?"

Hubert gave a sigh of frustration but still did not look up. "Is there a certain time you two talk?"

"Usually around nine," Scott answered.

"I tap into the bulletin board and record all phone calls at that time. You tell me which nights you talk, we compare the list, and bingo." He gave another loud sniff to indicate the problem was solved.

Darryl sniffed back in confirmation.

Hubert sniffed one last time, as if to have the last word.

Scott was obviously impressed with this new form of communication, but he still had one more question. "What about the address?"

Hubert sighed his best Why-am-I-sur-rounded-by-morons? sigh. "Obviously, I run a trace on his number and find out where he lives."

"Hubert," Darryl exclaimed, "you're a genius!"

"Yeah?" Hubert asked. "So what's your point?"

Darryl shrugged. Apparently he had none.

"Make sure the door locks on your way out."

~

Meanwhile, back at the house, Mom was exhausted. The last few weeks had been rough on her. Real rough. Besides helping the kids adjust to their new surroundings (Crescent Bay, California, was just a little different from Jungleland, Brazil), she was also pounding the pavement, looking for work. It had been another long day of driving, filling out applications, and hearing the all-too-familiar "Sorry, no openings. Why don't you try again next month?"

She had barely dragged herself up the porch steps and entered the door when Becka grabbed her, sat her down on the sofa, and explained that they'd be having company any minute. Mom wasn't thrilled about the idea of a strange man coming into the house. She was even less pleased after Rebecca told her all that had happened at the library the night before. Granted, Mom didn't know much about reincarnation, but what she did know made her nervous. As she listened to Becka, little alarms began to go off inside her head. The same alarms she'd heard whenever villagers back in Brazil shared stories about witch doctors and black magic.

But those alarms were interrupted by another sound: the doorbell.

"It's him!" Becka exclaimed as she jumped up and dashed out of the room.

"Where are you going?"

"I gotta brush my hair!"

Mom shook her head as she wearily rose and crossed to the door. When she opened it, she was caught completely off guard. She had expected some sort of strange and eccentric-looking weirdo. What she saw was a tall, handsome man with thick silver hair, who was dressed in stylish khaki slacks, a turtleneck, and a sport coat.

He looked positively respectable. And gorgeous.

"Mrs. Williams?"

"Y-yes?" Mom stuttered.

"I'm Maxwell Hunter."

"Yes, uh, we were expecting you." It wasn't until she looked into his warm, masculine eyes that Mom realized she hadn't changed or freshened up or even combed her hair. She looked exactly like she felt . . . a mess. But there was something in the way Maxwell held her gaze that said he saw past the mess, that he understood her day's trials, and, as amazing as it may seem, that he was actually attracted to the person underneath the frazzled exterior.

She liked him instantly. And with that liking came guilt. After all, the man wasn't here for her. He was here to talk about Becka. Besides, how could she be feeling such things for another man? Her husband had been dead only six months.

Yet wasn't she human? Wasn't she at least entitled to appreciate another man's company?

As though understanding her struggle, Hunter smiled gently. "May I come in?"

"Oh yes, of course." Mom blushed slightly

and opened the door for him. As he entered she found herself smoothing the wrinkles in her dress.

"What a lovely home you have, Mrs. Williams."

"Oh, well thank you, but it still needs, well, it needs lots of work. The tenants who used to live here were . . ." Her voice trailed off.

"Strange?" he finished for her with an amused twinkle in his eyes.

"Well yes, how did you know?"

He slowly surveyed the room. "Sometimes . . . I just sense these things." He turned back to Mom and smiled warmly. "I sense lots of things."

She glanced away. Had he "sensed" what she was thinking about him? Or was he just flirting? Whatever the case, for the first time in a long time, she suddenly felt attractive, flattered, and nervous all at once.

"Ah," he said, turning toward the kitchen, "there she is."

Becka had just entered the room. She was carefully eyeing her mother. Again Mom flushed. Had Becka also read her mind?

"Your mother and I were just discussing the past tenants of this house."

"Yeah," Becka agreed. "You should see the stuff out in the garage."

Maxwell turned in the direction of the garage and paused as if listening to something. Becka and Mom glanced at each other.

"There's something out there that disturbs you?" It was part question, part statement.

Becka and Mom looked at each other again. Each knew the other was thinking about the strange noises and the dancing light Becka had seen in the garage several nights earlier.

"Yes, well." Mom tried to change the subject. "I'm sure it's nothing. Won't you have a seat?"

He nodded and eased himself onto the sofa. "I am certain you have many questions and are probably more than a little skeptical." He turned to Becka. "But may I ask one question first?"

Becka shrugged. "Sure."

"Your dreams last night, were they disturbing?" Once again his eyes locked onto hers, and once again, they seemed to be looking inside her.

"Well . . . yes." She fidgeted. "They were a little weird."

He smiled. "I thought as much. Let me come straight to the point." He turned to Mom. "I believe your daughter—in fact, your entire family—has some very unique gifts. And I believe many of these gifts come from past lives, from who you were in other eras."

Mom looked down and cleared her throat.

"Please." He smiled. "Don't be embarrassed. I know you don't believe me. I'd recognize that tone of throat-clearing anywhere."

They chuckled lightly.

"It's not that." Mom paused, looking for a diplomatic way out. "It's just . . . well, we're both Christians and—"

"So am I," he broke in with a grin. "I knew we shared common ground. I sensed it."

"You're a Christian?" Becka asked.

"Absolutely. I believe Jesus was the Christ prophesied throughout all of Scripture."

"So you believe in the Bible?" Mom asked.

"Certainly. It is one of the most holy books we have."

A wave of relief swept over the two women. "Good," Mom said. "I'm glad we have that cleared up."

"Yes indeed." Maxwell nodded. "That is very important. You see, what I am proposing is not contradictory to Scripture. Not at all."

Mom continued to watch him. If what he said was true, then her concerns should be calmed. But the alarms were still ringing in her head. He leaned forward and touched her arm gently, growing more sincere. "I know it all seems strange. The truth often sounds outrageous. Just look at how the disciples reacted to Jesus when he told them things they didn't expect. They also were confused. It took them a long time to really understand what he was saying."

The man seemed so sincere, so genuine, that Mom found herself wanting to believe him. He smiled, and as he looked at her, Mom could swear there was a real honesty in his eyes.

"I understand your hesitation. You're a good mother, and you're just protecting your daughter."

His words continued to comfort her . . . no, it wasn't just comfort she felt. There was something else. What was it about this man that made her feel so . . . good?

"Mrs. Williams, I want to protect Rebecca too. Believe me, I don't want to harm her in any way. But I believe your daughter has led a powerful life in the past, and with your permission, I would like to help her unlock that power to assist her in this present. Not to hurt her but to help her. Isn't that what we both want? To help her?"

Mom held his gaze. The alarms were growing quieter. "How?" she asked.

He leaned back. "Hypnotism. Nothing strange. No hocus-pocus. Just the simple clearing of your daughter's mind—helping her push aside distracting thoughts so her past memories may surface."

Mom hesitated. "I don't know. . . ."

"I understand your concern. That is why I felt it would be best to do it here in your own home, under your supervision."

"You want to do it here? Now?"

"Only with your permission." His voice remained calm and reassuring. "And under your careful scrutiny. If for any reason you feel the slightest bit uncomfortable, we will stop immediately. You need simply say the word."

Mom continued to hesitate. "I'm not sure. . . ." She looked at Becka.

"Of course," he added, "we will pray together before we begin and ask God to guide us."

A wave of relief swept over Mom. If he was willing to pray with them, wasn't that proof that he was genuine in his faith? She paused, then looked again at Becka. "Sweetheart, what do you say?"

Becka swallowed. "Will it be scary . . . you know, like the last time?"

"No." He shook his head firmly. "That was your death. We will skip past that and go

53

directly to earlier years. We will discover your powers of the past, which will allow you to utilize them in the present."

Mom shifted slightly as she watched Becka thinking it over. Despite Maxwell's calm words, she still felt a little anxious. She wished her husband were here. He had always been able to see things more clearly, to see past the surface to the truth. But he wasn't here. He would never be here again.

At last Becka spoke. "I think . . . it would be OK." She turned to Mom. "I mean, you'll be right here to watch." She looked to Maxwell. "And she can stop it any time?"

Maxwell nodded. "Any time."

Mom turned to her daughter. "Are you sure?"

Becka slowly nodded.

"It's really that important to you?"

Becka shrugged. "I don't know if it's important. But it would be kinda neat, don't you think?"

Mom looked at her daughter a long moment. Finally she nodded. "OK, Sweetheart . . . if it's what you want."

"Good." Maxwell clasped his hands together in approval. "You won't regret this, Mrs. Williams. I assure you."

Mom tried to smile, hoping he was right. "So, what exactly do we do?

"Do you have a candle and some matches?" he asked.

"Yes, in the kitchen."

"If you would bring them in."

"Certainly." Mom rose and headed into the kitchen, once again straightening her dress and, this time, also smoothing her hair.

"And Becka, if you will just get comfortable in that chair over there." He pointed to the overstuffed chair near the window. "We will set the lighted candle on this coffee table, here, and get started."

Mom entered with the matches and candle.

"Thank you," he said. As he took them, their hands brushed slightly and their eyes met. He held her gaze for a moment, and Mom glanced to the carpet, once again feeling her face flush.

Maxwell positioned the candle and its holder on the table. He smiled at them reassuringly. "Let's all pray now, quietly, and ask God to guide us." They bowed their heads.

"O high god," he said, "we ask you to help us—to show us the perfect path to greater enlightenment."

There was a moment's pause, and then the sound of a match being struck. Mom and Becka opened their eyes. Apparently the prayer was over, for as they looked up they saw Maxwell touch the flame to the candle. It flared brightly, and their gazes locked onto his. He smiled.

"Let us begin."

4

*B*ecka concen-
trated on the candle's flame, on seeing nothing but its pure, white light and hearing
nothing but Maxwell's soothing, calm voice.

"Put aside your thoughts. Think only of
your breathing. In . . . and out . . . in . . . and
out . . . in and out . . ."

Gradually her eyes closed. She focused on

her breathing, listening to it, feeling it, making it her only thought. Once again she began to float . . . to fall gently. Once again there was that strange feeling of detachment as she drifted backward through layers of burgundy reds.

"What do you see?" Maxwell's voice was far away. "Do you see any light?"

Becka began searching the colors.

"No, don't look," Maxwell ordered. "Don't force it to appear. Let the light emerge on its own."

She relaxed. Gradually, it appeared directly in front of and slightly above her.

"Yes," she whispered, "I see it. It looks like . . . it looks like a star."

"Excellent," Maxwell's voice cooed. "Let it approach, let it draw you in."

It came closer and closer. Becka noticed a tiny, pinpoint hole in the center. As the star approached, the hole grew larger. Soon she saw that it was an opening, a type of doorway. It drew closer, continuing to grow. But as it did so, Becka began to feel uncomfortable. A cold fear stirred somewhere inside her.

"Let go, Rebecca," Maxwell's voice encouraged, "let it approach."

As the hole grew, so did her fear. "I—I can't. . . ."

"Let go, Rebecca. Let it have its way. . . ."

"I—" She tried to relax, but the fear was just too great.

"It's OK, then," Maxwell soothed. "Another time . . . another time . . ."

The opening and its surrounding light faded as quickly as they had appeared.

Instantly Becka heard sounds. Human voices screaming and shouting in French. Once again the shapes and shadows of the platform, the soldiers, and the crowd appeared.

"No!" Becka gasped. "I'm back at the guillotine!"

She heard her mother's voice but couldn't make out the words. Then Maxwell broke in, peaceful, in control. "Let them go. Let those images wash over you. Go back farther, go deeper."

Rebecca forced herself to relax, and sure enough, the images shifted and flickered. The screaming mob and surrounding soldiers shimmered and waved until they became towering trees.

"I'm in some sort of forest," she whispered.

"Good, good," Maxwell said. "Look around you. Tell me what you see, what you feel."

"I feel movement. The ground is shak— no, wait. It's not the ground. I'm on a horse. I'm on a horse, and we're trotting through woods. I hear men talking and dogs barking. I think . . . it looks like a hunting party."

"That is marvelous, Rebecca, just marvelous. Look down at yourself. Tell me what you are wearing."

Becka looked to her hands. She could see them holding the horse's reins. She was surprised at all the rings she wore—there must have been half a dozen. She was also surprised to see the silks, lace, and the white furs draped across her arms. But what really shocked Becka were the hands. They were strong and large. . . .

Becka gasped. "I'm a man!"

She heard Maxwell chuckle. "I suspected as much. Look about you, what else do you see?"

Becka looked around the forest. There were men on horses ahead of her and behind her. Their clothes were nice but not nearly as elegant as hers.

And then she saw them. On the ground. A handful of peasants dressed in rags dropping to their knees and bowing their heads as she passed.

"They're bowing—people are bowing. Maxwell, am I, like . . . royalty?"

"Look back to your hands. Do you see any rings?"

"Yeah, plenty."

"On your right hand—do you see one large ring with letters on it?"

Becka looked to her right hand and saw a large gold ring with writing. "Yes, it has letters and numbers—Roman numerals."

"Read them!" Even though his voice was far away, she could hear his excitement. "Read the numbers. What do they say?"

She obeyed, "There's an *X* and a *V* and an *I.*"

"That's sixteen! Are you sure you're reading a sixteen?"

"Well, yeah. What's that supposed to mean?"

"Are you sure it's sixteen?"

"Yes. Why is that such a big—"

But her question was cut off by another voice, a different one than Maxwell's—a voice filled with alarm.

"Becka!" It was Scott. "What are you doing to her!"

Now she felt somebody shaking her.

"Becka, wake up! Becka!"

The ring started to fade, and then the hand.

"No," she whispered, "not yet. Not—"

More shaking. Harder. "Becka, wake up! Come out of it! Wake up!" Scott's voice was much louder.

"Scotty . . ."—that was Mom—"You don't underst—"

Becka felt herself returning to the over-stuffed chair in the living room.

"Becka . . . BECKA!"

Her eyes fluttered open. There was Scott, shouting into her face. Behind him stood Mom. Then Maxwell.

"What do you think you're doing?" Becka croaked. Her voice was dry and raspy. And angry. Very, very angry.

~

Half an hour later, Scott sat up in his room, steaming. How was he supposed to know what they were doing? When he had entered the living room, all he saw was some gray-haired goon leaning over his sister, getting all excited about the number sixteen. How could he know this was something Becka wanted to do? How could he know this was something she had *already* done?

Hypnotism . . . reincarnation . . . Scott shook his head. What was going on?

He was mad. No doubt about it. Mad that Becka hadn't told him about last night. Mad that she was mad at him. And mad at the gray-haired goon. Maxwell.

Besides giving Scott the scare of his life, the guy claimed Becka might have been some sort of powerful king in some sort of past life.

Puh-leeze, Scott thought. *Past life? King? Give me a major break!*

And if that wasn't enough, ol' Maxy boy had asked Mom if he could call her sometime. Call her? *His mom?* The guy was practically asking for a date right there in front of her own kids! What gall!

Scott didn't like him. Not one bit. And this whole thing about reincarnation. How could his sister believe that? Wasn't reincarnation some sort of Hindu thing? And weren't the three of them supposed to be Christians? Christians didn't believe in reincarnation . . . did they?

He glanced at the radio alarm clock near his bed. A wadded up T-shirt hung over the front, but he could still make out the time: 9:02.

He angrily snapped on his computer and dialed up the bulletin board. Maybe Z would be around. After giving his password and switching over to the "Chat" line, he typed:

Anybody home?
Good evening, New Kid.

Remembering his arrangement with Darryl's cousin, Scott grabbed a pencil and wrote down the date and time. As he did, more words appeared:

I heard what happened to Rebecca last night at the library.

Great! Everyone knew but me! So what do you know about reincarnation? Is it a Christian thing?

Z's response was slow and measured:

If you are Christian, reincarnation is directly opposed to what you believe.

How?

Reincarnation teaches that you die again and again and keep coming back until you are finally good enough to enter heaven. Your Bible clearly states that people are destined to die once and after that to face judgment. That's in a book of the Bible called Hebrews, chapter 9, verse 27.

"I knew there was something fishy about it," Scott muttered. But deep inside he was a little disappointed. He was hoping for more than just one Bible verse. He typed:

Is that it? Isn't there anything else?

Reincarnation teaches that the only way to get rid of your sins is to live several lifetimes until you work them out. Christ teaches that he paid the price for your sins when he died on the cross.

So?

So . . . those who believe in reincarnation are saying they don't need Christ. They believe they can work their way into heaven on their own.

Scott mulled this over a moment. Z was right. It didn't get any more basic than Jesus dying on the cross. But what about Rebecca's experiences? What about seeing herself as some king?

What about the all the stuff Becka is seeing when she is hypnoti—
New Kid, somebody is tapping into our line.

Scott went cold. He knew who that somebody was, but he also knew he had to play dumb.

What are you talking about?
Somebody is listening. I must go.
I still have more questions.
Good night.

And that was it. Z had signed off.

Scott stared at the screen. Z sounded frightened. Scott wondered if he'd done the right thing, trying to track him down. There was a gnawing feeling inside that maybe he hadn't.

~

"A mighty king . . . incredible greatness . . . Unlock your secret powers. . . ."
Maxwell's words tumbled through Becka's

65

mind as she lay in bed, trying to sleep. What type of powers? What type of greatness? And what about that star with the opening inside—why was that so frightening? Maxwell wouldn't say. No matter how much she pleaded, he would not tell her. As he'd left the house that evening, his only words were that she should keep listening to her dreams, that the power would eventually reveal itself.

Becka wasn't sure when she finally drifted to sleep—or when all the tumbling words and thoughts finally solidified into a dream. She only knew it was night . . . and that she was standing on some sort of hill or ridge. There were no stars, no wind, no sounds.

She glanced down. Once again she was robed in the silks and furs of royalty. Twenty or so feet below the ridge was a path where she saw the students from her school. Like the peasants in her vision, they were all kneeling on the ground, bowing before her. Julie, Ryan, friends from the lunch table—even the two seniors who had passed her in the hall—they all had their heads lowered in honor and respect.

Becka shifted, embarrassed over the attention. She wanted to call down to them, to tell them to get up, to stop making such a fuss. But then she saw it, directly ahead. She sucked in her breath. It was the star from her vision. And it was moving quickly along the ridge, coming directly at her!

With its approach came a low rumbling that grew louder and louder—a thundering so powerful that it shook the ground beneath her feet.

Becka looked back down to her friends. They began rising, concern filling their faces.

She turned back to the approaching star. It was growing into a blazing light, brighter than the sun. The thundering had turned into a roar that filled her ears.

"Run!" the kids shouted. "Get out of the way!" Ryan started scrambling up the ridge. "Becka!" he screamed. "BECKA!" But his friends pulled him back.

The light was practically on top of her now. She could feel its power surging against her, pulsating, beckoning her. Again she saw the dark hole in the center, and again she felt the icy fear as the opening grew. She tried to push the fear aside. There was power here, waiting for her. Why should she be afraid of it? But as the hole grew, her fear increased. Now the hole was the size of a small tunnel, a passageway that led to the very center of the light. She saw nothing else. Just the blinding light of the star—and the darkness of the tunnel.

Fear turned to panic. Light was everywhere, enveloping her, enfolding her, sucking her into the tunnel, its center. But the more it pulled, the more she struggled, until finally, gasping for breath . . .

Becka awoke.

She lay in bed, staring at the ceiling, chest still heaving . . . and felt outrage at her cowardice. Twice now she had refused the light. Twice now her fear of the unknown had prevented her from entering the tunnel, kept her from experiencing its power. And it *was* a power. She knew it. She had felt it.

She glanced at the clock radio: 5:07.

She still had a good couple of hours before school, but that was OK. She reached over and snapped on the bedside lamp. Becka Williams didn't plan on going back to sleep.

5

It felt kinda weird for Rebecca to be at the breakfast table before Scott. After all, he was the morning person. The Mr. In-Your-Face-with-the-Jokes-before-You-Had-the-Chance-to-Wake-Up. But there she was, encyclopedias spread all over the kitchen table, reading away.

"How long have you been up?" Scott

asked as he shuffled into the room. He crossed to the cupboard and grabbed his faithful box of Kix. Next stop was the refrigerator for milk and then the dishwasher for a clean bowl and spoon. It was the same routine every morning. He could do it in his sleep. Sometimes he did.

"I've been up 'bout an hour," Becka answered as she continued reading.

Scott plopped down at the table and pushed aside a couple of the books to make room for his stuff. "What's all this?"

Becka knew he wouldn't like the answer, but she also knew she couldn't hide it from him. "I'm reading up on reincarnation."

"Don't tell me you buy that garbage."

His attitude irritated her, but she pretended not to notice. "I'm not buying into anything. I'm just checking on a few facts, that's all."

Scott snorted in disgust and poured his cereal.

She continued, trying to be casual. "Did you know that over half of the world believes in reincarnation? And so does one out of every four Americans?"

"So?"

"So it's considered to be the fairest and most just belief system in the world."

He looked up. "What?"

She read from the book, "'Reincarnation teaches that each individual is punished or rewarded for their deeds. If one is evil in a past life, he will suffer in the next. If he is good, he will be rewarded.'"

"Tell that to Z."

She glanced up from the book. "You talked to him?"

Scott poured the milk over his cereal. "Last night. He says reincarnation is a total joke."

Another wave of resentment washed over Becka. "Maybe Z isn't an expert in everything."

"I'm just telling you what he said."

"He can say whatever he wants, but he can't say I didn't see what I saw."

Scott shrugged. "He also said you can't believe in reincarnation and be a Christian."

That was it. Becka had had enough. "That's exactly what I'm talking about—he doesn't know everything. Mom and I asked Maxwell if he believed in the Bible, and the guy said yes, absolutely, one hundred percent. He believes in Jesus, and he even prayed with us before the hypnotism. Got that, Scotty? The man prayed with us."

Scott stared. For once in his life, he had no comeback.

"Morning, guys." Mom breezed into the

kitchen. Her tone was so cheery that both kids looked over at her. She opened the bread, pulled out a couple of slices, and dropped them into the toaster. Was it their imagination, or was she humming? Then there were her clothes. She wore her pink-and-orange flowered dress, one of her favorites. And her hair—it had been months since either of them had seen it so carefully brushed and sprayed.

"What are you all decked out for?" Scott asked.

Mom stood at the sink, filling a coffee mug with water. She crossed over to the microwave and set it inside. "Not a thing," she answered as she punched in the time and hit Start. The oven gave a little beep and began to whir.

Becka broke into a mischievous smile. "Wouldn't have anything to do with Maxwell Hunter, would it?"

"Of course not," Mom said, catching her own reflection in the window and adjusting her bangs.

"Oh, please," Scott moaned.

"What's your problem?" Mom asked.

"I think he's just jealous," Becka offered. "He doesn't like you dating good-looking studs."

"If he calls up, you're not really going to go out with him, are you?" Scott whined.

"Knock it off," Mom chided, "both of you. Just because a person takes a little care in their looks doesn't mean they're suddenly jumping into the dating scene."

"You didn't answer my question," Scott said.

Mom put the loaf of bread away and resumed humming.

Becka looked down to her book with a knowing smile.

"If you ask me," Scott said as he shoved another spoonful of cereal into his mouth, "I think the guy's totally bogus."

"Really?" Becka pretended to question.

"Oh, yeah, you read about those type of fakes all the time."

Perfect. He'd set himself up. Becka went in for the kill. "Well, it just might interest you to know that that 'fake' knew all about the noises and light in the garage."

Scott stopped chewing. The noise in the garage had been a mystery to the three of them ever since they moved in. They figured it was somehow connected to the weird boxes the last renters had left behind, but they couldn't be sure. It was an eerie screeching sound that came at the most unpredictable times. And to top it off, just last week, when Becka was investigating it, she'd thrown open the door connecting the kitchen and the garage and had seen a mysterious light flit across the room.

Of course, none of them believed the sound and light were supernatural or anything, but for some reason they'd been keeping the door to the garage locked . . . and for some other reason they only went out there when they absolutely had to.

Becka felt calm and reassured. Twice she had been able to shut down Scotty's arguments. Maybe this was part of the power Maxwell had promised—the "unlocking of secret talents." She didn't know, but it felt great. It was time to change the subject. "Can Ryan pick me up after track practice?" she asked.

"Will you come straight home?"

"We might swing by the east side. He's a big brother to one of the kids over there."

The microwave chimed. Mom removed the mug of hot water and headed for the cupboard to dump in a teaspoon of instant coffee. "Ryan seems like a nice boy."

"He's better than nice, Mom. Even you would approve."

Mom smiled. "I'd better."

Becka continued, "The guy's so sweet, you wouldn't believe it."

"Oh, *please!*" Scott groaned for the second time. He rose, crossed to the sink, and rinsed his bowl. He didn't say another word. He just headed out of the room and back upstairs to get ready for school.

Becka watched. She wasn't entirely sure what his problem was, but she expected it had to do with Maxwell. Why? What about Maxwell Hunter made Scott so angry?

~

"We got him." Darryl scooted beside Scott at the cafeteria table.

"Got who?" Scott asked.

"Z. You guys talked last night, didn't you— around nine?"

"Yeah."

"So we got him." Darryl pushed up his glasses and gave a heartier-than-usual sniff.

Scott looked on with distaste as the kid swallowed. He was getting pretty used to the sniffs and snorts. But not the real loud ones . . . and not while he was eating. He glanced at the vanilla pudding cup in his hands and thought he'd wait a minute before digging in.

Darryl hadn't noticed a thing. "My cousin called up with his address this morning."

"You're kidding! That fast?"

Darryl reached into his shirt pocket and pulled out a folded piece of paper. "I told you he was good." He handed the paper to Scott. Now, at last, they could discover who Z was. Maybe uncover how he knew so much. And most important, maybe they could find out why he had taken such an interest in Scott's family.

And yet, with all of those possibilities, Scott hesitated. He could not unfold the paper.

"What's wrong?" Darryl asked.

"I don't know. . . ."

Darryl gave his glasses another push.

"The guy was pretty spooked last night," Scott said. "I mean, he knew when your cousin tapped into our conversation, and he hung up right away."

"So?"

"So he obviously wants his privacy."

"What's that got to do with anything? He'll never know we know."

Scott nodded. "But, still . . ."

"Hey, Williams."

He turned to see one of the members of the Society passing by the table. It was the big, meaty guy in the tank top—the same tank top he wore nearly every day. Luckily he wasn't looking for a fight. In fact, he almost sounded friendly. "I heard about your sister," he called as he moved toward the exit. "Pretty cool. Let her know we're rooting for her."

Scott nodded but did not smile. The fact

that the Society thought Rebecca's experiences were "cool" didn't exactly thrill him. And what did the guy mean, they were "rooting for her"?

"Are you going to open it or what?" Darryl asked.

Scott was still thinking about his sister.

"Scott." Darryl sniffed again, loud enough to bring Scott back to reality. "If you want, we can track him down and pay him a visit as early as tonight."

Scott looked back to the folded paper in his hand. "Tonight?" his voice croaked.

"Sure." Darryl shrugged. "Why not?"

Scott raised a finger to his mouth and began chewing a nail. Why not, indeed?

~

At track practice Becka's mind was barely on her running. In fact, Coach Simmons had shouted at her more times than she could count. "Come on, Williams. Focus! FOCUS!"

Becka tried, but there were just too many things on her mind. Funny, a week ago running was all she thought about. But now . . . well, now things were changing.

"Everything OK?" Julie asked as they toweled off in the locker room after their showers.

"Huh?" Becka looked up a little startled.

"Are you all right?"

"Oh, yeah . . . sure." Becka forced a smile and reached for her sweatshirt.

Julie watched her carefully. "Ryan's waiting outside."

"Great!" Becka said as she finished dressing, grabbed her things, and headed off. "We'll see you tomorrow."

"Yeah . . . ," Julie said slowly. "Tomorrow." She watched as Becka disappeared around the lockers. There was no missing the concern on her face.

~

"Come on, pretty lady, it's 8:08. Hurry up!" Pepe tugged at Becka's hand as they scrambled up the grade toward the train trestle. The loose gravel slipped under her feet, slowing her process, but at Pepe's insistence, she pressed on.

Ryan was right behind them. "You sure this is safe?" he asked.

"Sure I'm sure," Pepe said. "I do it all the time. We won't even be on the tracks, I promise."

Ryan had made it clear that he wasn't crazy about visiting the Death Bridge. But ever since they'd arrived, it was all Pepe had talked about. And he assured them again and again it would be perfectly safe.

The thought of being this close to the spot where so many kids had been killed should have given Becka the creeps. But, for some reason, she felt a faint attraction toward the place. It probably was just morbid curiosity. But Becka sensed there was more to it than that.

At last they reached the top of the grade. Becka let out a gasp. She had been here before! Last night . . . this was the ridge she'd stood on in her dream! Only now there was a train trestle just ahead and tracks that continued another hundred yards before disappearing around the bend. Other than that, it was identical to her dream. Becka was certain of it.

For a moment all three stood looking on in silence. And, for a moment, all three thought of the crazy, half-drunk teenagers who had been batted off of the trestle like flies or crushed under the train's merciless wheels.

"Come on." Pepe tugged at Becka's hand, urging them to follow him onto the trestle.

"No way, amigo," Ryan said. "This is far enough."

"I don't mean we stand on the tracks. I mean we stand over there." Pepe pointed to the outside girder of the trestle, a steel beam with plenty of room to walk.

"Pass," was all Ryan said.

Pepe shrugged and looked to Becka. She also shook her head. He let go of her hand and started toward the trestle.

"Pepe!" Ryan warned.

"I do it all the time, *mi hijo*. Don't worry." He reached the trestle and stepped onto the steel girder.

"But—"

"You're sounding like my mother." He grinned. "Don't worry."

Becka and Ryan watched as Pepe tight-rope-walked the steel beam—effortlessly working his way along the outside of the bridge. From his position it was clear there was no way a train could hit him. Of course if he slipped and fell, he could bash his brains out on the road twenty feet below. But with all the handgrips and footholds, that didn't seem likely.

"Be careful," Ryan warned.

"Relax," Pepe called. "It's no biggie."

"Just be careful."

As Rebecca watched she felt a strange detachment creep over her. The same detachment she felt when she was being hypnotized. Suddenly it was as if things weren't completely real. As if they weren't that important. If Pepe remained safe on the trestle, fine, he deserved it. If he slipped and

fell, that would be OK, too, because he probably deserved that. It was as if everything was
part of a plan . . . the workings of a "fair and
just universe."

She turned and looked out over the neigh-
borhood. Here, high atop the grade, she
could see everything. The pathetic houses,
the broken-down cars, the ragged children
playing in the street. But this time she felt
no heaviness. This time she felt very little
pity or compassion. Only detachment. All
this poverty, did it really matter? If reincarnation was true, then this was justice—people
simply paying for how they had lived in the
past. Why should she feel sorry for them if
they were getting what they deserved?

The thought struck her as strange and yet
perfectly logical. But before she could think
it through, she heard a faint rumbling.

"What's that?" Ryan asked.

"It's the train!" Pepe called over his shoulder. By now he was halfway across the steel
beam. "It's the 8:10—right on time."

"Get off there!" Ryan's voice was sharp
and full of concern. "Come on! Get off
there!"

Pepe laughed.

"Pepe!"

"Don't worry, amigo! I do this all the
time!"

"Get off there now!"

"I'm perfectly safe!" Pepe called. "But you two, you'd better climb down."

Becka and Ryan looked up the tracks to the bend. They saw nothing, but they could feel the ground vibrate as the rumbling grew louder.

"PEPE!" Ryan cried.

"Go on!" Pepe shouted. "Get down. It will be here any second!"

Ryan stood frozen, unsure whether to go out and try to get the boy or to head down the grade with Becka.

"Come on," Becka said. "He'll be OK."

Ryan looked to her. How could she be so sure? Granted, Pepe was on the outside of the bridge, far from the train, but still . . . how could she be so sure?

"It'll be OK," she repeated and took his hand. "Come on."

At last the train rounded the bend. Its bright headlamp cut through the night fog, flooding their faces, forcing them to squint. Its rumbling grew louder. Suddenly it blew its whistle—a shrill and piercing warning.

"Come on!" Becka pulled at Ryan and, at last, he followed. They slid down the steep gravel grade. The rumbling had turned to a roar—a roar so powerful it filled their ears and vibrated their bodies.

They did not look back but continued sliding down the grade.

By now the roar was deafening. Halfway down, safely out of reach, Becka suddenly released Ryan's hand and spun back to the train . . . just in time to see the locomotive thunder past. The wind hit her face and blew her hair. The ground pounded. The roar filled her body.

Over on the trestle, Pepe clung to the outside beam, laughing and shouting.

Becka didn't notice. She closed her eyes to savor the moment—the pounding, the thundering, the roaring. It was here. The same power she had experienced in the dream. It was exhilarating. Overpowering. Before she knew it, she also began to laugh. Like Pepe. Only harder. She gulped in the air, reveling in the power. A power she could practically taste. A power she knew would be hers.

6

So how do I look?" Mom asked Becka for the twentieth time.

"You look great."

"You sure?"

"Trust me."

Becka wiped down the kitchen counter while Mom loaded stray cups and dishes into the dishwasher. Scott was out with Darryl, tracking down Z, and that was just fine with Becka and Mom. They were about to receive a guest—a guest they both knew Scott wasn't crazy about. Maxwell Hunter had just finished another lecture and would be arriving any minute to pick up Mom for a late-night dinner.

"What if we don't have anything to talk about?" Mom asked as she poured the soap into the dishwasher and closed it.

"Ask him about himself—guys always like that."

"How do you know?"

"That's what you always told me!" Becka laughed.

"Oh, right," Mom chuckled. "That's how I caught your father." Suddenly she turned to Becka. "You don't think I'm betraying him, do you—your father, I mean?"

The question brought Becka up short. Not because she hadn't thought of it, but because ever since she learned Maxwell had called, it was all she had thought of. Becka missed her father. Desperately. People had said the pain would go away, but they were wrong. It had been six months since his plane had crashed in the deep jungles of Brazil, but sometimes it felt like six minutes. The ache would never leave. She knew it.

But she knew something else too. She

knew Mom could not go on living life alone.
Oh sure, she was a strong lady and could
make it on her own—with God's help, of
course. She'd been doing just that for a lot
of months now. But Becka could see how
much Mom missed the sharing, the support,
the closeness she and Dad had always had.
Mom needed someone she could love—and
someone who would love her—the way she
and Dad had loved each other. And as much
as it hurt Becka to think of another man
married to her mother, she was pretty sure
someday it would happen.

"I think it's great!" she lied. "I'm sure
Daddy would think so, too."

Mom searched Becka's eyes, grateful for
the words but somehow sensing the lie.

The doorbell rang.

"It's him!" Another wave of panic hit
Mom, which of course led to more dress
smoothing and hair adjusting.

Becka grabbed the coat on the chair and
slipped it over Mom's shoulders. "You look
great. . . . Stop worrying." She turned her
mother toward the door and gave a little
push. "Go."

With the added momentum, Mom
headed for the entrance hall. She checked
herself in the mirror one last time, then
opened the door.

Maxwell stood on the porch. He wore a gold turtleneck sweater under a tweed sport coat. In his hands were a dozen roses. "Hello, Mrs. Williams."

Mom stood speechless.

Becka waited for her to say something, but nothing was coming from Mom's mouth. Finally the word *hi* squeaked out—a little too loud, a little too hoarse.

Becka winced. Suddenly she understood where her own clumsiness with boys came from. It was hereditary. Like varicose veins.

Maxwell handed Mom the roses, and she gave the obligatory "Oh . . . they're beautiful."

Maxwell smiled, then spotted Becka standing in the background. "Good evening, Rebecca."

"Hi." She smiled.

"How are your dreams?"

Her smile faded. She tried to answer but only managed to give a shrug.

"Listen to them very carefully. They will unlock your power."

"You know, don't you?" Becka asked. "You know who I was, and you know about this power." She hadn't planned to bring up the subject—this was Mom's night. But the guy had started it. "Why can't you just tell me?"

Maxwell's smile broadened.

Becka continued. "When I saw the number sixteen on my ring, you got all excited. You know who I was."

"Listen to your dreams," Maxwell repeated. "Once you know your past, it will unlock the power of your future."

"Why won't you just tell me?"

"When the time is right, you will know."

Rebecca sighed in frustration.

"Becky," Mom said, trying to change the subject, "would you put these in some water for me? There's a vase up in the—"

"If you don't mind," Maxwell interrupted. "I would prefer you to keep these this evening."

Mom looked at him a little surprised.

He explained. "Their beauty only reflects the greater depth of your own."

Becka had never seen Mom blush, but there was no missing the color running to her cheeks. "Well . . . all right," she fumbled. "If that's what you want."

Becka smiled. It was kind of cute.

"Our reservations are at nine," Maxwell said, reaching for the door. "I am afraid we must be on our way." He opened the door and allowed Mom to pass.

"Have a good time," Becka said.

"Thanks," Mom called back.

Maxwell hesitated, then slowly turned to Becka. "You, too, Rebecca Williams. This evening will have surprises. Be sure to enjoy them." He gave her a knowing smile, then stepped outside and shut the door.

Becka stared at the closed door. A little puzzled . . . and a lot unnerved.

～

Scott and Darryl rode their bikes down the secluded road. It was another foggy evening. There were no lights except for a soft moon whose edges were blurred by the fog. The dampness collected on Scott's handlebars and seeped through his jacket.

It had been half an hour since they rode out of town. Oh sure, there was still the occasional house and barking dog, but on the whole, things were definitely getting on the deserted side.

"You sure you know where we're going?" Scott asked.

"Absolutely." Darryl gave a loud sniff. The moisture didn't help his sinuses much. "Potrero Road. It's just around this corner, up here."

"That's what you said for the last three corners," Scott complained.

"Then we must be getting close."

Finally a tract of half-built houses appeared to the left in the moonlight. They were constructed back when everybody was moving to California and buying new homes. But now they just sat there, month after month—bare wood frames waiting to be completed.

As the guys approached a street leading into the complex, Darryl read the sign. "Potrero Road. See, I told you," he squeaked.

They turned off the pavement and onto a dirt road. It was strange. Everywhere they looked, they were surrounded by the bare skeleton houses. Stranger still was the fact that Z would choose to live in a place like this.

"Ohhh Darryllllll . . . ," Scott goaded.

Darryl pulled the paper from his pocket and read. "'Potrero Road.' It says right here, '1750 Potrero Road.'"

"Right," Scott nodded. "I see two basic problems: One, nobody lives here. Two, there aren't even addresses on the houses. Now, call it a wild guess, but maybe, just maybe, your cousin screwed up."

Darryl scowled, then sniffed. "I don't get it," he squeaked. "Hubert never makes mistakes . . . not like this. Maybe there's—"

Suddenly a security patrol car pulled around the corner and approached them. In a true, hospitable fashion, the driver snapped on his searchlight and shone it directly into their eyes, purposely blinding them.

"Hey!" Darryl shouted. "Turn that off!"

Scott said nothing as he tried to shield his own eyes.

The car pulled beside them and stopped. But the light never left their faces. It remained directly on them, so bright they were unable to see the driver.

"What are you kids doing out here?" The voice was coarse and gruff—anything but friendly.

"We're looking for somebody," Darryl answered with a definite attitude.

"You're what?" the voice sounded even tougher.

Scott stepped in. One of his specialities was diplomacy, defusing tense situations. He cranked up his smile to about 9.9 and did his best to sound friendly. "We're looking for 1750 Potrero Roa—"

"Nobody lives out here," the voice snapped. So much for diplomacy. "These houses are all vacant."

"But we have the address right here," Darryl protested. "It says—"

"This here's private property, kid. So get your rear ends outta here 'fore I have you arrested."

"Nobody lives out here at all?" Scott asked, giving diplomacy one last shot while trying to see past the light to the driver.

"Does it look like it? Now, move it."

Darryl argued, "Hey, it's a free—"

"Get outta here 'fore I throw you out!"

"Yeah," Darryl demanded. "You and who—"

Scott interrupted. "We're on our way, mister. Sorry to bother you." He gave Darryl a look that said, "I'm not in the mood to have my face turned into pizza topping by some gorilla security guard."

Darryl took the cue. Reluctantly he followed Scott as they turned their bikes around and headed back toward the main road. Unable to resist, Darryl shouted over his shoulder, "Have a nice day!"

The driver said nothing. He remained at the curb and followed them with the searchlight until they were out of sight.

Rebecca was obsessed.

No matter how hard she tried to concentrate on her homework, her thoughts kept drifting back to Maxwell's words. They weren't idle chatter—she knew that. And he wasn't a fake—she knew that too. Her visions had been real. So was the power she had experienced in her dream—and the power she'd felt beside that train. She was somebody great. She knew it. Somebody with extraordinary powers and talents that were trying to surface from within.

But who? Who had she been?

She'd tried praying about it, but her

prayer had felt strange, empty . . . like there was no one at the other end. So once again the encyclopedias were out—scattered all over the living room floor.

First she had tried to look up *guillotine*. That was her original vision, back on the stage in the library when she was about to have her head cut off. But she wasn't sure how to spell it and tried half a dozen different ways before finally giving up.

She slammed the book shut and reached for the dictionary. Maybe that would be easier. As she flipped through the pages she thought of the age-old question *If I knew how to spell it, why would I need to look it up?*

After another half-dozen tries, she finally found the word.

guillotine: a machine for beheading by means of a heavy blade that slides down in vertical guides

"Wonderful," she sighed. "I've already figured that out." But at least she had the spelling. She turned to the encyclopedia and tried looking it up.

GUILLOTINE, French method of beheading; a blade between two posts falls, when a supporting cord is released, onto the vic-

tim's neck below. The guillotine came
into use in response to J. I. Guillotin's call
for a more humane form of execution.
Last known public use: in France in 1977.

"More humane?" Becka mumbled.
"They've got to be kidding!"

Well, all that told her was that her vision
could have taken place anytime before 1977.
With a frustrated sigh, Becka set the book
aside.

Now what?

She remembered the soldiers with the
long bayonets. But they used those things
just about everywhere in the seventeen or
eighteen hundreds.

OK, what about the screaming mob?

Again, no clues. *If I could only make out
what they were saying,* she thought. But since it
was in French, she had no idea what they—

"Wait a minute!" she exclaimed. "French!
Of course!" If they were speaking French,
chances are it happened in France. And if it
was a French guillotine . . .

She struck her forehead, once again
astounded by her incredible lack of intelli-
gence.

She grabbed the "F" encyclopedia and
turned to "France"—past the people section,
past the government section, past the maps,

past the tourist attractions, over to the history section. If she was a great king, she would surely be mentioned in the history section.

Unfortunately the history section was over sixty pages long.

"Great . . . I'll be here all night." She flipped through the pages, glancing at pictures, drawings, headings . . . and then she saw it. A sketch of a guillotine! Her eyes shot to the caption which read: "Method of execution used during the French Revolution."

Becka's heart started pounding. She turned to "French Revolution" and started reading in detail—all about the dates, the leaders, the actions. It wasn't until she'd plowed through the fifth or sixth page that she saw it. Then she could only stare.

There, in front of her, was a portrait of a man. A man dressed in the same flowing materials she had worn—the same silks, the same furs, the same lace.

She looked to his face. It was heavier than hers, but there was no missing the eyes. They were *her* eyes. She was certain of it. She was looking at herself!

Finally, she glanced to the caption. It simply read: "Louis XVI, king of France."

Becka closed her eyes. She could feel the power tugging at her—washing over her. It was all there . . . a king, France, and the Roman numeral sixteen. Rebecca Williams had been Louis XVI!

She took a deep breath and opened her eyes. She found his section and read on.

She read how Louis . . . no, how *she* had tried to be a good king, how she was compassionate toward the poor peasants, how she loved hunting (which explained her vision on horseback with the dogs). She read how she was well-meaning but too trusting—too kind and inexperienced. And she read how those latter qualities led her to make wrong decisions, which eventually led her to be executed. By the guillotine.

Everything was there . . . Becka Williams . . . compassionate, kind, trusting to a fault. And, most importantly, king of the most powerful nation on earth.

She took another trembling breath. But she wasn't shaking with fear. She was shaking with excitement. And power. She had been a king. A great king. True, she had had one weakness. Her kindness and gullibility. But now she knew. And with that knowledge and the power of her past, imagine what she could become today!

Scott entered his room and peeled off his jacket. Cornelius was dozing on his perch, so the kid didn't bother turning on the light.

It was late and he was tired. As far as he could tell, Mom and Becky had both gone to bed early. At least their lights were off.

He undressed, snapped on his computer, called up the bulletin board, and checked for any messages.

There was one.

He clicked his mouse and paged down to read:

> I heard you stopped by. Sorry to miss you. How about tomorrow night, 7:00, same place? Z

Scott shuddered and stared at the screen. How could Z have known?

7

It had been a long time since Mom had felt so protected, so secure, so . . . *cared for.* Ever since her husband had died, she'd been the one who had to take control. The one forced to run the show. Of course, the kids did their part, but the final responsibility always rested on her shoulders.

Until tonight. Because tonight, Maxwell Hunter was in charge.

From the flowers to the Italian restaurant (complete with a violin player) to the maître d' who doted on her slightest whim—every detail of the evening had been taken care of. And it felt wonderful.

Maxwell Hunter radiated power—and tonight, that power seemed absolutely devoted to her. As the evening progressed, Mom found herself growing more and more attracted . . . but at the same time, there was still the slightest trace of caution. It was a strange yet pleasant mixture of emotions: attraction and caution.

It took nearly an hour for the small talk to drift to Maxwell's faith. "So, when exactly did you become a Christian?" Mom asked.

Maxwell smiled as he poured the remainder of the wine from the bottle into his glass. He wasn't drunk, but he was definitely relaxed. Very, very relaxed. Once again he offered some to Mom, and once again she politely refused.

"When did I become a Christian? Well now, that's difficult to say. I think I first became aware of the Christ within sometime during my sophomore or junior year of college."

"I'm sorry?" Mom asked, "'the Christ

within'? . . . You mean, that's when you received Christ?"

Maxwell smiled. "Yes and no. You see, he's always been inside. I just didn't experience him until then."

Mom was confused. "What do you mean, 'He's always been inside'?"

"I mean, each of us have the Christ living inside—" he took another sip of wine and continued— "from the moment we are first born."

Ever so faintly, the alarms Mom had heard when they first met began to sound again. "You mean," she gently corrected, "Christ comes inside, once we ask him to forgive us of our sins."

Maxwell chuckled. His eyes were growing moist, taking on the dull sheen of someone who was slowly but steadily getting drunk. "Sin. Now there's a quaint notion. Sin is a state of mind. We all have the Christ inside. We're all sons of the most high. It just takes some of us longer to tap into that power than others."

"Power?" Mom shifted slightly. The alarms grew louder.

"Yes." Maxwell nodded. "We are all Christ. We all have his power." Before Mom could respond, he glanced around the restaurant and lowered his voice. "Would you like to see that power?"

Mom simply looked at him.

"Watch." He fumbled with a spoon beside his plate. It may have been the wine or just a little clumsiness, but it seemed to take him a while to pick up the spoon and set it on the white tablecloth between them. When he had, he stretched out his index fingers and placed one at each end of the spoon—not touching it, but very, very close.

Mom watched uneasily. When she glanced up at Maxwell, he was grinning—like a schoolboy about to play a prank. Ever so slowly, he raised his index fingers. They never touched the spoon. But as he raised his hands, the spoon followed, lifting off the table . . . one, two, four inches high.

Mom continued to stare. Her uneasiness had turned to fear. The alarms were going off strongly now. Full volume. Whatever power this man had was definitely not from the Lord. "I . . . uh," she pulled the napkin from her lap and stood. "I think we'd better call it an evening."

Maxwell looked up at her in surprise, and the spoon suddenly fell to the table with a loud clatter. He looked at it, startled, and then back at her with an almost hurt expression. "Why did you do that?"

Mom shifted uneasily. "I think you'd better take me home."

Three minutes later, Mom strode as fast as she could along the outside of the building toward the back parking lot. Maxwell was several yards behind, shouting, "Will you please wait up!"

As she passed the garbage bin, she noticed a black and brown stray dog. He was so busy scrounging for food that he didn't see her, but for some reason, as Maxwell passed, the dog suddenly lifted his head, his ears pricked. He spun around, letting out a harsh growl.

Maxwell looked at the animal, surprised.

Mom glanced over her shoulder.

The dog drew back his upper lip, snarling—the deep, guttural growl coming from deep inside his chest.

Maxwell slowed to a stop.

Mom also slowed. As much as she wanted to avoid this man, she didn't want to see him hurt. "Just keep walking," she called. "He won't attack if you let him be."

But Maxwell didn't seem to hear her. He was concentrating on the dog.

"Maxwell?"

As Mom watched, the man's stare seemed to intensify, until it became a menacing glare—a glare as fierce as the dog's.

Mom felt a cold shiver spread over her. It was unnerving, as if the man and dog were entering some sort of unspoken, but formidable, standoff. Mom heard another growl—but this time she could swear it came from Maxwell.

"Maxwell?"

He still didn't seem to hear. His gaze was fixed on the dog.

"Maxwell."

Finally the dog made his move. He crouched down, taking two tentative steps, preparing to attack.

Mom stepped forward in alarm. "Maxwell, look out! He's—" But she never finished the sentence, for suddenly Maxwell pointed his arm directly at the dog and shouted in some unintelligible language.

The dog yelped and was thrown to the pavement, whimpering in pain.

"Maxwell! What are you doing?"

As she watched Maxwell with growing alarm, it seemed as if someone or something had taken control of him. He continued glaring at the dog, which seemed to increase its pain, making it writhe in agony. The beast's whining was only interrupted by an occasional pain-filled howl.

"Stop it!" Mom shouted. "You're hurting him!"

"Wrong, my dear," Maxwell mumbled in a strange, flat tone as he continued glaring at the pathetic animal. "I'm not hurting him. Not at all." A faint smile crossed his face. "I'm killing him."

The dog lay on his side now, his tongue rolling out, the panting and whining growing weaker, more pathetic.

Horrified at what she was seeing, Mom screamed at Maxwell. "Stop it!"

But Maxwell would not listen. He actually seemed to take pleasure in the creature's pain.

Without thinking, Mom rushed at him, hitting him with her small purse. "Stop it! I said, stop it!"

The unearthly glare suddenly vanished from Maxwell's face. He glanced around, confused, disoriented. Immediately the dog's whimperings stopped, and it struggled shakily to its feet. Mom wasn't sure who looked more baffled by what had just happened, the dog or Maxwell. The pitiful animal licked his chops, gave a final uncertain whine, then quickly slinked away, stealing into the dark shadows of the alley.

Maxwell turned to Mom. "What . . . what happened?" He sounded lost, almost helpless.

Mom stepped back. She wasn't sure what she had witnessed, but she was sure she had seen enough.

Maxwell saw the fear in her eyes and forced a smile. "It's all right," he said, trying to sound in control. "I can explain. I can explain everything."

But Mom was in no mood for an explanation. Any more than she was in the mood to be anywhere near this man. She turned and started to run.

"Wait! Please, I can explain!"

But Mom did not wait. She did not reply. She just kept running. All she wanted was to get away—from Maxwell, from whatever evil this was—and to get home so she could warn her little girl.

Rebecca dreamed.

She had put away the encyclopedias and had gone to bed early for that specific purpose. Maxwell had said the evening would hold surprises. He had been right so far. Maybe there were more.

Soon she was standing on the train trestle. Again everything was still. No wind. No stars. Just a thick fog. Below her, the loyal friends and subjects were on their knees, bowing their faces to the ground.

Becka adjusted her fur robe and straightened the lace of her sleeves. This time she was not embarrassed. This time she knew why they bowed. It was her birthright. Her destiny.

The ground under her feet began to vibrate. She looked toward the bend up ahead and waited. Any second, the star would appear. And with it, the power. She was frightened, but she was also excited. She had failed twice—but this time she would not back down. She would let the power have its way.

A faint rumbling began . . . and grew.

The students below looked at each other. Some began rising to their feet in alarm, but Becka was not worried. She knew their minds could not understand what was happening; they could not comprehend the power she was about to experience.

The rumbling expanded into a roar. Suddenly the star pierced the darkness. But this time it was more than a star. It was also the headlight of the train.

The crowd panicked, but Becka wasn't surprised. The train, the star, the power . . . somehow they were all connected. Soon she would be a part of that connection.

The train thundered toward her. She could feel its energy. Its whistle cut through the night, but she did not move. This time she would not back down.

"Becka!" Ryan shouted. "Becka, run!"

Becka barely heard. She looked into the approaching light. It blazed brighter and brighter, filling more and more of her vision. And with it, directly in the center, was the tunnel . . . the passageway. Again her fear rose, but this time she was able to push it aside, for, as the light continued its approach, its energy began flowing into her, filling her, empowering her.

Then she saw him . . . inside the tunnel. In the center of the power stood Maxwell Hunter. It was impossible to see his face, but there was no mistaking his silhouetted sport coat and beard.

The power roared in her ears, filling her head, flooding her body. The tunnel grew wider—wide enough to enter.

Fear tried to stir within her. *"Be careful,"* it whispered. But as Maxwell reached out his hand to her, motioning for her to join him, the whisper faded away.

She saw no train now—only light. Finally she understood. The *light* held the power. And if she could feel this much power outside of the light, imagine what intensity awaited her inside.

She raised her arms toward Maxwell. He continued holding his hand out to her as they drew closer and closer. Their hands were just a few yards apart now, when suddenly—

Becka awoke.

Once again she was breathing hard. Once again she was covered with sweat. And once again she was angry that she could not go further. Why? What was preventing her from entering the light?

She rolled over and looked at her clock: 11:33.

Then she heard a muffled noise. Straining to listen, she realized it was footsteps. Up and down the hall they paced. Back and forth. And murmurings. Quiet but anxious murmurings.

Still angry at being awakened and still feeling the power of the light, Becka threw her feet over the side of the bed and went to investigate. She had no fear as she crossed to the door and threw it open.

A shadowed form turned to confront her.

"Mom?"

Her mother was pacing back and forth, head bowed. She still wore her evening dress and coat.

"Mom, what are you doing?"

The woman looked up, startled. "Oh, Becky." She ran to her daughter and threw her arms around her.

"What's wrong?" Becka asked. "What are you doing?"

"He's evil, Becka. Whatever he's doing, we must stay away from him."

"Who is? What are you talking about?"

"Maxwell Hunter!"

Becka felt herself stiffen. She was not prepared to hear this. Not from her mother. Not after all the power she had just experienced. "Why? What happened? Did he make a pass at you?"

"No, it's more than that." Her voice shook slightly, and she drew a deep breath. "Becky, he's involved in the occult. I'm sure of that much now."

Becka grew defensive. Maxwell was a good man. She knew it. Look at the power he had unlocked inside her, the power that was just waiting to be hers. She started to speak, but one look at Mom told her she was too worked up to reason with—at least for now. So Becka tried to change the subject. "What are you doing out here, pacing back and forth?"

Her mother held her look for a long moment. Finally she answered. "I was praying, Becky. I was praying that whatever we got ourselves into, God would forgive us. That whatever influence Maxwell may have over you would be broken."

Rebecca's anger flared. How could her mother be so ignorant? Just because she didn't understand Maxwell's powers didn't make him evil! Mysterious, yes. But not evil!

And Becka was angry for anther reason. Suddenly she knew, without a doubt, that it had not been her mother's pacing that had awakened her. She knew it had been her mother's prayers. That's what had stopped the dream. That's what had prevented her from stepping into the tunnel of light.

It was her mother's careless, superstitious prayers that had prevented her from experiencing the power that was waiting for her.

$\sim$

At school the following day, Rebecca's attitude was no different. Finally she knew who she was and the power that would soon be hers. All she had to do was endure the ignorance of those surrounding her.

She was sitting at a table in the library, poring over a book when she heard, "Missed you at lunch."

She glanced up. "Oh, hi, Julie."

Julie pulled out a chair and sat. "Can I talk to you a sec?"

"Well, I'm kinda busy—"

"What are you reading?" Before Becka could answer, Julie spun the book around on the table and read, *"Modern Day Hinduism.* What's that about?"

Becka turned the book back and said, "I'm afraid it's too complicated for you to understand." She hadn't intended to hurt Julie's feelings, but she had succeeded all the same.

Julie scowled slightly. "Beck, can I be honest?"

"Sure."

"Some of the kids are saying—not me, of course—but the others, they say you're getting, like, a major attitude."

"What do you mean?"

"Well, after that hypnotism thing . . . it's like, I don't know . . . it's like these last couple of days you're thinking you're better than the rest of us."

Becka just stared. How immature. How petty. Of *course* she was better. She had been a king, a powerful ruler. But that was only the beginning. Soon she would be experiencing even greater powers. Becka wanted to explain all this, but she knew it would be pointless. So, instead of explaining, she played dumb. "What do you mean?"

Julie took a deep breath. But before she could answer, Ryan strolled in. "Hey, Beck." He gave his usual grin. "We missed you at lunch."

"Yeah, well I had a little research to do."

"You going with me to Pepe's after track practice?"

"Uh . . . I don't think . . ." Becka hesitated.

She knew they wouldn't understand, but she had to tell them. "I won't be staying for track tonight."

"You what?" Julie asked in surprise. "Beck, we have the state meet coming up."

"I know, it's just—well, I have some other more important things to do."

"More important than State?"

Becka looked down at the table and shrugged. She'd known it would be pointless.

Julie and Ryan exchanged glances.

"Well, uh . . . " Ryan cleared his throat. "Maybe I could pick you up later, at home, and we could swing by Pepe's this evening." He forced a gentle laugh. "If you ask me, I think he's really got a crush on you."

"Maybe I'll go," Becka said as she glanced at her watch. There were only a few minutes left of lunch. Funny, a week ago she would have died for the opportunity to go to the state meet or to spend any time with Ryan. But now . . . now she just wished they'd both leave so she could get back to work.

"I can't explain it . . . " Apparently Ryan was still talking about Pepe. "But when we hang around him, it kinda gives him hope— like maybe he can get out of there someday."

Becka hesitated, wondering if her friends could understand what she was about to say. There was only one way to find out. "Ryan, have you ever thought that . . . well, that maybe Pepe is living where he is for a reason?"

"What do you mean?"

"There's this thing called karma." She nodded toward the book on the table. "It's like the justice you create for yourself, and then you carry it around wherever you go. If you've been good in the past, if you have good karma, you'll be rewarded, like in future lives. If you've been bad, then your karma will be bad and you will be punished."

"What's that got to do with helping Pepe?"

She tried again. "What if by helping Pepe, you're really hurting him? What if you're just messing up the justice of the universe so he has to come back and suffer all over again?"

Ryan frowned. "Run that past me again?"

Becka glanced to Julie. She looked equally confused. Becka had been right. Her friends wouldn't understand. But then how could she expect them to? After all, they hadn't experienced what she had. She tried one last time. "What I'm saying is—"

The bell rang to end lunch. Becka felt a wave of relief. "Oh well." She smiled. "It's just a theory." She closed the book and started to rise. "Maybe we'll get into it again some time." She gathered her stuff and headed for the desk to check out the book.

Of course she knew Julie and Ryan were staring after her, but she didn't hold it against them. It wasn't their fault they didn't know. It wasn't their fault they didn't understand. Nobody understood. Not Scott, not Mom, not her friends. Nobody.

Nobody but she herself. And, of course, Maxwell.

The skeleton houses loomed on both sides as Scott and Darryl pedaled down Potrero Road. It was 7 P.M.—the time Z had asked for the meeting.

Though neither boy would admit it, their hearts both pounded.

Ever since Scott and Becka had moved to Crescent Bay, Z had been a mystery. He seemed to know everything about them . . . and he seemed to know everything about the occult. Why? Was it the occult that gave him his powers? Was it the occult that told him Becka's name and the other half-dozen things he knew but had never been told? Perhaps. But if he was involved in the occult, then why would he spend so much time warning them about it? None of it made sense.

But it would. Soon. Very soon.

A set of car headlights rounded the corner. Scott and Darryl recognized them instantly.

"Uh-oh," Scott groaned. "It's Mr. Hospitality."

The security patrol car headed directly toward them.

"Here we go again," Darryl muttered.

But this time there was no bright light glaring in their eyes. This time they were able to clearly see the driver. He was a plump man in his sixties. He pulled up alongside them and rolled down his window. Reluctantly Scott and Darryl slowed to a stop.

His voice was no more friendly than the night before. "You're late."

Suddenly Scott's heart sank. Could this be him—could this be Z?

Before either boy had a chance to respond, the driver continued. "Follow this road for two more blocks. After the second cross street, it's the fourth house on your right."

Scott's mouth dropped open. He thought he heard himself saying, "Thanks," but he wasn't sure. In any case, the guard didn't answer. He simply rolled up his window, pulled away, and continued down the street.

Scott and Darryl looked at each other in

amazement. But they didn't say a word.
What could they say? As always, whenever
they dealt with Z, there was a surprise.

They pedaled down the road of deserted
structures in total silence. At last the house
came into view. It had to be the one. No
question. It was the only house with a car
parked in front. A white Jaguar.

They slowed, hopped their bikes over the
curb, and stopped on what would someday
be the front lawn. Like all the other houses,
this one only had bare studs for walls and
bare rafters for a roof.

Scott and Darryl glanced at each other
one final time. Silently they set their bikes
down and started toward the house. They
could see nobody inside. There was no light,
no movement.

They stopped at what was supposed to be
the front entrance.

"Hello?" Scott called.

No answer.

"Hello?" he repeated. "Anybody home?"

"Knock, knock," Darryl called.

Suddenly, deep inside the house, an
orange light flared. Someone had struck a
match. For the briefest second they saw the
glow of a man's face lighting a cigarette. He
was small and had long dark hair.

"Hi, there," Scott called, trying his best to

sound casual. He might have succeeded if his voice hadn't cracked. But it always tended to do that when he was scared out of his mind.

"Over here," the voice called. Scott and Darryl froze in astonishment. It was the voice of a woman!

She was only a shadow among the other shadows. A shadow . . . and a faint glow of a cigarette.

Darryl and Scott stepped into the house and headed toward her.

8

Z? Is that you?"
Scott called as they moved through the
house toward the shadowy form.

There was no answer. Only the brightened
glow of the cigarette as the woman took
another long drag. She tilted her head back
and blew the smoke out impatiently.

The guys continued forward. "Are you Z?"
Scott repeated.

"Don't be ridiculous." Her voice was thick and raspy.

As they approached, they could see she was seated on a wooden sawhorse. She was small, almost tiny, and her feet barely touched the ground. She kept her head in the shadows so it was impossible to make out any detail of her face. But the moonlight struck the cloud of smoke behind her, making it glow, creating an eerie silhouette of her nose, chin, and hair.

They slowed to a stop. Once again the cigarette grew brighter as she took a long drag. Scott cleared his throat. "We were supposed to meet somebody here. His name is—"

"I know," the voice cut him off. She leaned forward, momentarily bringing her face out of the shadows. She was dark complexioned, maybe Hispanic. "Z could not come. I am a friend of his. I owe him a great deal." Her accent was not Spanish but Asian. Maybe from India.

"So you've met him." Scott stepped a little closer.

The woman chuckled. "Yes, I have met him."

"Well, could you . . . I mean, who is he? Could you tell us how he knows so much about—"

"There are some things that are better for

you not to know." She took a final drag from the cigarette, dropped it to the floor, and crushed it out. Scott's mind raced. He had heard that exact phrase from Z just the other day.

"There are some things that are better for you not to know."

"But who—"

"It is your sister that should be your concern."

Scott tensed. "How do you know about my sister?"

"I know nothing about your sister except that she is dabbling in something about which she is ignorant."

"Dabbling? In what?"

"Reincarnation."

"Hold it." Darryl sniffed a little irritably. "Are you telling me Z brought us all the way out here just so you could tell us about his sister?"

Scott agreed. "I know Becky's reading up on all that junk, but it's really not that big of a—"

"Maxwell Hunter is a well-known proponent of hypnotic regression and channeling." She paused, then continued. "His methods can be most dangerous."

"Dangerous?" Scott repeated. "What do you mean?"

The woman gave no answer.

Scott continued. "Reincarnation is—well, just a belief. Of course it's not true, but there's nothing wrong with believing in something, just because it's not tr—"

The woman interrupted. "I am a victim of that belief."

The answer brought Scott up short. "Victim?"

"My name is Nagaina. I was born in Nepal, a mountainous country north of India. My parents were killed in an earthquake when I was only seven."

"I'm sorry. But what's that got to do with—"

"My village was Hindu, which meant we believed in reincarnation. Because my parents were killed, I was thought to be cursed by the gods. I was believed to have been an evil person in my former life."

"That stinks," Darryl offered.

The woman nodded. "For my own good, I was cast out of my village and left to die. They believed the more quickly I died and paid for my past evil, the more quickly I would be reincarnated into a better life."

"You mean nobody would help you?" Scott asked.

"They were afraid to interfere with my karma, to incur the wrath of our gods."

"So . . . ," Scott said slowly, "you not only

lost your parents, but you were thrown out
of your village and left to die."

The woman nodded. "When your—" she
stopped and started again. "When Z found
me, I was dying in the woods, so starved that
I was eating dirt to fill my stomach."

"All because your village believed in reincarnation?"

She nodded. "On the surface it seems
innocent, almost plausible. But as you follow
reincarnation to its logical conclusion, you
will see inhuman treatment, indifference to
suffering, and little respect for human life."

There was a long pause as Scott and Darryl digested the facts. Finally Scott spoke.
"And you're telling us all this because . . . ?"

"Z is greatly concerned for your sister."

"Because she's playing with reincarnation?"

"And because she is associating with Maxwell Hunter, who is an acclaimed Eastern
mystic. A man who uses the forces of hell to
ensnare his victims."

Scott gave an involuntary shudder.
"'Forces of hell'? Those are some pretty
strong words."

"They are truth." The woman glanced at
her watch and rose to her feet. "It is late. I
must go."

"Wait a minute, where are you going?

How can we get in touch with you if we need—"

"You will not see me again." She produced another cigarette and struck another match.

"But . . . what if, what if we need to get a hold of you or something?"

She drew the smoke in deeply, then blew out the match as she exhaled. "I have done this as a favor for Z. He is a great man. I owe him much. But I think we shall not meet again, Scott Williams." She dropped the match to the floor and moved through the skeleton house toward her car.

Becka didn't know how long she sat on the bed in her room. All she knew was that she was getting sick of fighting with Scott and Mom about Maxwell Hunter. Of course, she knew they were under a lot of pressure—especially Mom, what with moving into a new town, getting everyone situated, having to be both mother and father. Of course, she didn't want to add to that pressure. But that didn't give Mom the right to try and stop something she knew nothing about.

Maxwell Hunter was a good man. In just a few short days, he had given Becka the self-confidence she had always lacked. He had freed her from the old Rebecca Williams—

the shy, self-conscious little loser who always blended into the background. That Rebecca was dead. And with the help of Maxwell, the new Rebecca was being born. Soon she would be leaving obscurity and rising toward the greatness destined to be hers.

It might have been easier if Maxwell wasn't friends with the folks at the Ascension Bookshop. And it didn't help that he sometimes acted a little weird. But that couldn't dismiss Becka's experiences or the revelation of who she was or the incredible power beckoning to her.

Mom had said she would not let Becka see Maxwell again. She had made that crystal clear as they fought and argued over their dinner of macaroni and cheese. But no more Maxwell meant no more hypnotism. Which meant no more clues. Becka sat in silent frustration. Then, slowly, gently, a thought crept into her mind.

Maybe . . . maybe Becka didn't really need him. The book she had checked out of the school library—and that she'd been reading all evening—said she could obtain the same state of "higher consciousness" she'd experienced in hypnotism on her own. It was just a matter of relaxing and "clearing one's mind."

Weren't those the exact same words Maxwell had used?

She flipped to the page of a woman practicing this "higher state." Following the example of the picture, she crossed her legs, sat up straight, and touched the middle finger of each hand to its opposing thumb. So far so good. Now it was just a matter of relaxing and "clearing her mind."

Easier said than done. It seemed every time she closed her eyes, a thousand thoughts tumbled in. Without someone like Maxwell to direct her, it would be very difficult.

Difficult but not impossible. It could be done. The book said so. She sat there, trying again and again until, gradually, she was able to push aside her thoughts and concentrate only on her breathing. . . .

In . . . and out . . . in . . . and out . . .

Slowly she emptied her mind.

In . . . and out . . . in . . . and out . . .

Until every thought was gone. Now her mind was empty, a blank slate. There was only her breathing.

In . . . and out . . . in . . . and out . . . and the now-familiar sensation of falling backward through layer after layer of color.

It could have been minutes; it could have been hours. She wasn't sure. But, slowly, the light appeared. It hovered in front of her and above. When she looked at it, it would fade. But when she stared straight ahead, keeping her mind empty and not forcing it, the energy grew brighter and brighter until it was finally so strong she knew it was no longer just inside her head. She knew the light had somehow entered the room!

She opened her eyes.

Yes! There it was! Just above the foot of her bed. It continued to brighten. As its energy increased, so did its power. Becka could feel it blowing against her face. But it did more than blow. As it touched her face, she could feel it saturate her body.

Once again a dark passageway formed in the center. And once again she saw a man.

Maxwell.

He turned to her and smiled. She smiled back.

The light grew. It filled the entire room. She could feel the power invading her, surging through her body. She started to laugh. She couldn't help herself. The feeling was too pure, too intense.

Maxwell laughed too.

From inside the tunnel, he reached his hand out to her. This time there would be no interruptions. This time she would take his hand and the power would finally be hers . . . she would be absorbed into it, and it would be absorbed into her. The two would become one. And with that oneness would come such energy, such strength, that no one would ever doubt her again. She would belong to power, and the power would belong to her.

Becka raised her arm toward Maxwell. The energy surged. It had a sound. A roar. Like the train. She could feel and hear it thundering inside her.

Their hands drew closer, fingers nearly touching. She was losing control. Good. Finally, she would be able to give herself over to the power. Completely. Without reservation.

But something stopped her. A noise. A . . . knocking. Banging.

"Becky! Becky! Open up!" More pounding. "Becky, open up!" It was her mother.

No! Not again!

She threw a quick glance at the door. The light dimmed.

No! Don't go! She focused back on it.

"Beck!" A different voice. "Beck, it's Scott. We gotta talk!"

She felt Maxwell's irritation, his displeasure. He began to withdraw his hand.

"No!" Becky cried.

He hesitated.

She reached out both of her hands. *"Please?"* she begged. "Please!"

128

There were a series of crashes at the door. Scotty was obviously trying to break in.

"Please," Becka repeated, rising to her knees, reaching toward the light.

It grew brighter. Maxwell began to smile.

"Becky! *Becky!*"

She barely heard.

Maxwell reached out his hand.

"BECK!"

Closer and closer they came.

"BECKY!!"

At last they touched. The power swept into her, enveloping her. She gasped. Her eyes fluttered. She was losing consciousness, being pulled into the center.

Suddenly the door exploded open.

9

*B*eck!" Scott raced into the room. Mom was right behind.

The light disappeared. The power vanished.

Becka turned on them furiously. "I was there! I had it!"

"Had what?" Mom asked. Her eyes fearfully searched Becka's.

Rebecca glared at her in contempt. The woman was so ignorant, so superstitious. But before she could answer, Scott jumped in. "I just talked to a friend of Z's. Mom's right about this reincarnation stuff. It's wrong—real wrong. And this Maxwell guy, he's like some sort of—"

"I know exactly who he is," Rebecca snapped. "He's a man with more power than your little mind can possibly understand."

"Becka!" Mom scolded.

"Well, it's true. Just because you don't understand something doesn't make it wrong."

"Maybe so . . . ," Scott agreed, "but this guy's bad news, Becky. And his power's flat-out wrong."

She rose from her bed and stepped to the other side, keeping it between them. "What do you know about power?" she demanded. "Have you ever felt it? Have you ever experienced it?"

"Becky," her mother took a step forward. "It's not just the—"

"I was king! King of France!"

"Becky—"

"And that's only the beginning. There's more for me—more than you can comprehend!"

"But it's counterfeit!" Scott was practically shouting.

The phrase struck Becka in the chest. She turned on him. "It's what?"

"Maxwell Hunter's into the occult. He's a major-league player in Eastern mysticism."

Becka started to tremble. Not with fear but with rage. Why were they doing this to her? She'd finally found something, a way to be somebody, and now they were trying to take it away. "You're just jealous!" she scorned. "You're jealous 'cause I experienced something and you—"

"Honey," Mom interrupted. "Just because you've experienced something doesn't make it—"

"I *saw* things! I was there! I was Louis XVI!"

"They were illusions," Scott argued. "They were hallucinations that couldn't possibly be—"

"They were *not* hallucinations! They were real!" Becka's eyes started to fill with tears. Why was he doing this? Why was he taking away the only power she'd ever had? "I saw things! I saw things only a person who had lived back then would know!"

"Only a person living then . . . ," Scott said quietly, "or a demon."

"What?!" She couldn't believe her ears.

"It's just like the Ouija board, Beck. The board knew stuff, remember? From different places, different times. It knew stuff, not because it had supernatural powers of its own, but because of the demons controlling it. The demons who had actually been at those places, who had actually seen those things."

A sneer curled Becka's lips. "*I* saw those things. Not Maxwell. Not demons. But *me!* I saw them."

"With Maxwell's help."

Becka would not cave in. "What about my dreams? On my own bed? Here, in my own room!"

"Dreams you had after Maxwell hypnotized you."

"What's that got to—"

"Dreams are cool," Scott continued. "They helped me remember all that stuff Dad tried to teach us. But—" He took a deep breath, and Becka knew she was going to hate this next thought even more. "Somehow . . . I don't know how, but somehow, you're letting Maxwell influence . . . even control you. Maxwell or . . . whatever critters he has with him are trying to—"

"You're telling me all this is done by demons?!" Becka shouted.

"Honey." Mom started toward her.

"What about my power?" Becka stepped back. "What about the light?"

Again Mom and Scott looked at each

other. This time they had no answer. This time Becka had them, and she knew it.

"Ha!" she mocked. "You don't know, do you? You don't know about the power. You don't know about the light. And you know why? Because you're not chosen. Because you haven't lived my past, you're not worthy of the power that's going to be mine. You're not ready for the light!"

"Becky," Mom said, approaching. "What power? What light are you talking about?"

Becka laughed. "I've experienced more power than you will ever know. And it's only the beginning. There's plenty more waiting for me. All I have to do is—"

"Becky." Scott edged closer.

She whirled at him. "You don't believe me?"

"I believe . . ." Scott chose his words carefully. "I believe you think you've experienced some sort of—"

"Think?!" she shouted. "You think I've just imagined all this?" Her mind raced. She had to show him, to make him eat his words. Suddenly an image filled her mind. The train. Its glaring headlight. The roaring engine, the thundering power. She didn't know where that image came from, but she knew what it meant. Of course! Let them witness it firsthand! She turned to Mom. "What time do you have?"

Mom glanced at her watch. "It's nearly eight. Why? What does that—"

"You have to take me somewhere."

"Becky, I don't think now's the—"

"If you take me somewhere, I can show you. I promise."

"Beck—"

"I promise. And if I'm wrong . . . If I'm wrong, then you can talk to me all you want and I'll listen."

Again Mom and Scott exchanged glances.

"But you've gotta let me show you first."

"Where?" Scott slowly asked.

"Not far. But we've got to hurry."

Mom and Scott hesitated, but not Becka. She snatched her sweatshirt off the bed. "Come on," she ordered. "You want proof; I'll show you proof!"

～

The van cut through the fog as it followed the road, dipped under the Death Bridge, and rose back up.

"Right here," Becka ordered.

"Here?" Mom asked doubtfully.

"Stop the car," Becka insisted. "We have to get out here!"

Mom slowed the van. Before it even came to a stop, Becka slid open the side door and jumped out.

"Becky!"

"Hurry," Becka called back. "We haven't much time!" She turned and started toward the grade leading up to the tracks. She couldn't explain the energy rushing through her body. Or its connection to the train. But she knew they were the same. And then there were Maxwell's words: *"To fully experience the power, you must let go; you must let it have its way."*

Finally, she was doing that. Finally, she had quit questioning. And as she did so, the power grew. The closer she came to the tracks, the more the urgency within her grew. Something was pushing her, driving her forward.

"Becky!" Mom called. "Becky, slow down!"

"We don't have time!" Becky shouted. She arrived at the grade leading up to the tracks. "Hurry!" Her feet slipped on the gravel as she scrambled up the hill, but she dug in and continued climbing.

Scotty was climbing right behind. "Beck! Becky, wait up!"

And then another voice, farther away. "Hey . . . Becka! Rebecca!" It was Ryan.

"Pretty lady, what are you doing?" And that, of course, was Ryan's little friend, Pepe. She'd almost forgotten. Ryan had said he was going to visit Pepe that evening. The two were probably nearby when they heard the shouting from her mother and brother. And now they were coming to investigate.

Perfect. Ryan can see this too.

She didn't look back, but kept climbing. When she reached the top of the grade, she quickly crossed to the center of the tracks. Already she could feel the faint vibration under her feet. The 8:10 was right on time.

"Becka!" She turned. Ryan and Pepe were closer now. She could almost make out their shapes through the fog as they ran down the road toward her. "Rebecca!"

She stared at them a moment, then redirected her attention back up to the tracks. To the bend. Everything was just as she had dreamed. Plenty of fog. No wind. No stars. Just an eerie stillness . . . and the distant vibration of the approaching train. Now she understood. *The dreams were just a preparation—a way of getting me ready for what was coming. But tonight . . . tonight will be the real thing.*

Scott arrived beside her, breathing hard from the climb. "What's going on?"

"Do you hear it?" Becka asked. She was also breathless, but more from excitement than exertion.

"Hear what?"

"Listen!"

There was a faint rumbling. Scott looked puzzled.

"It's the train," she said. "It'll be coming around that bend any second."

"What?" Scott asked in alarm.

"Becky!" Mom called from the bottom of the grade. She had tried to climb it, but it was too steep. "Sweetheart, what do you want? What do you want to show us?"

"Just stay there!" Becka called. "You'll see."

"See what?" Scott demanded. "What are you going to show us?"

Becka never turned to him. She just kept staring down the tracks. Her voice was hollow and empty. "You'd better get down, Scotty."

"What about you?"

Becka did not answer. The rumbling grew louder.

"Becky . . . what about you?"

"Rebecca!" Ryan's voice was much closer—practically under the trestle. Perfect, just like the dream.

"Becky?" Scott sounded frightened. "What about you?"

She didn't look at him but continued staring down the tracks. The rumbling had grown into a roar—an ominous roar. "You'd better get down," she repeated.

"Not without you." Scott took her arm.

"Let go."

His grip tightened. "Come on, we're getting outta here."

"I said let go." She tried to twist free.

"Not without—"

And then the train appeared. For a moment both Scott and Becka froze. Her heart pounded so hard she found it difficult to breathe. The headlight swept around the bend until it hit them squarely in their faces.

And with the light came the power. She could already feel its approaching energy.

"Come on!" Scott yelled. He pulled her hard, but she resisted.

"Let go!" she shouted.

"Beck!"

He grabbed her other arm and tried to pull, then push her off the tracks. She fought him. She was still just a little bigger, just a little stronger.

The train thundered toward them.

"Becky!" Mom shouted from below. "Scotty!"

But neither heard as they continued the fight. It was a bizarre sight—the two struggling up on the fog-shrouded tracks, lit only by the glaring light of the approaching train.

"BECKA!" Ryan arrived beneath the trestle. Pepe jumped up to the nearest girder and started climbing toward the tracks. Ryan raced to the hillside and started scampering up the grade.

As she fought her brother, the train's roar filled Becka's head. Everything was exactly like the dream. Exactly. She knew her power and the train's power were the same. They were one. She could not be hurt. She could only absorb the power and be absorbed by it. Everything was perfect . . . except for Scott.

She knew he was trying to help—to save her from the fate of the other kids who had played chicken up here and lost. But those were stupid pranks. Childish games. Kids who'd been destroyed because they weren't prepared. Because they weren't chosen.

She had to get rid of her brother. Finally she twisted one arm free.

The train blew its whistle—blasting, shrieking, screaming.

There was no other way. Becka was prepared. She could absorb the power. Scotty could not. With all of her strength, she leaned back and hit her brother in the stomach as hard as she could.

"OOOAFF!" he gasped as the air rushed out of him. He staggered backward until his heel caught the rail. He tripped and tried to regain his balance, but she was immediately there to push him the rest of the way. He fell and tumbled down the grade, rolling over and over, arms flailing.

"BECKY!" her mother screamed, but Becka did not hear. At last she was free.

She turned to face the blinding light. It filled her vision. She could feel the power encompass her. Her power. The power she had sensed so many times before. The power for which Maxwell had prepared her.

Once again the tunnel formed.

The whistle screamed, but she did not hear. Voices shouted, but she paid no attention. This was her moment. It was time to receive the power, to step into the light. She would become the power, and the power would become her.

Then she saw it. Movement out of the corner of her eye. "Rebecca!" It was Ryan. The fool was practically at the top of the grade, scrambling toward her!

She had no choice. She began to run. Straight toward the light.

"Rebecca!"

She arrived on the trestle and continued running. The light grew brighter. The center tunnel grew wider. Once again she saw Maxwell inside, reaching his hand to her.

The trestle jolted as the train reached the other side, pounding the tracks, shaking the steel girders.

Maxwell and the tunnel filled her vision. She could feel the wind, smell the diesel, hear the massive steel wheels on the tracks. She reached her arms toward Maxwell. As she ran, she tilted her head back, waiting for contact, waiting for the tunnel to swallow her and make her one. And at the peak of anticipation, at the moment of total freedom . . . she was struck.

But not by the train.

A small form had leapt off the bridge and almost knocked her out of the way. Almost, but not quite. A steel rail from the front of the locomotive caught both of them, flinging them off the bridge and into the gravel grade, sending them bouncing and rolling and tumbling down as the machine thundered past.

Becka remembered nothing after that. Only a blur of spinning sky and ground. And a small, dark-haired boy with blood spewing from his mouth and a look of horror frozen on his face.

Pepe.

And then there was nothing.

10

It was nearly three days before Becka started to remember. Oh sure, there were vague recollections of IV tubes, heart monitors, and concerned faces looking down at her. But nothing really came into focus until three days after the accident.

"Hey, Crash, welcome back." It was Scott.

He was grinning from the left side of the bed. As always, he was trying to lighten the moment.

Becka started to move, but the sudden throbbing in her head made it impossible. "Oooo . . . ," she groaned.

"Take it easy, sweetheart." It was Mom, leaning above her from the other side.

"Where am I . . . ," Becka mumbled. "What happened?"

"You played tag with a train and lost," Scott answered.

Becka groaned again as the memories rushed in. Memories of the Death Bridge, the train, the little form leaping at her from the side of the bridge. "What about Pepe?" She struggled to sit up. "That was Pepe who saved me. Is he OK?"

"Guess you'll have to ask him." Mom smiled as she glanced over her shoulder.

Pepe hobbled into view. His face was still pretty bruised, and the crutches made his movements a little jerky. But it didn't stop the smile. "Hello, pretty lady."

"Pepe! It's you!"

The boy grinned. "Mostly, it's me." He reached up and tapped his front teeth. "These are brand-new, though. Some sort of plastic. What do you think? Do they make me even more irresistible?"

146

"Pepe . . . I'm so sorry."

"No tenga pena," he said, shrugging. He threw a glance over to Scott and Mom. Realizing they'd want some time alone with Becka, he grinned at her. "Ryan's downstairs grabbing something to eat. He wanted to know as soon as you woke up. I'll get him and be right back." With that he turned and hobbled toward the door.

"Pepe?"

He stopped and turned back to her.

"Thanks," she said.

"For a lady of your beauty," he answered with a mischievous smile, "what else could I do?"

Becka couldn't help smiling back. The boy was a flirt to the end. He turned and headed out the door.

As she watched, more memories returned. It was as if she had awakened from a dream . . . a dream that began not long after her first experience in the library auditorium. She groaned. "I can't believe I was so stupid."

Mom and Scott exchanged glances.

"I'm just glad he's OK," she continued.

"Which is more than I can say for you," Mom answered. Becka looked up to her. "Concussion, broken collarbone, broken leg."

Becka looked down to her body to confirm the fact. Sure enough, she was wearing a few more casts and wires than the last time she remembered. She leaned back on her pillow and sighed. "What was I trying to prove?"

"I don't think it was just you," Scott said. "I think you had a little help from Maxwell and his buddies."

Becka turned to him.

He continued. "I had a long talk with Z. He said the junk you experienced with the light and power and stuff isn't all that unusual—especially for occultists. A little extreme, maybe, but nothing that unusual."

"By occultist, you're talking about Maxwell?"

Scott nodded. "Oh yeah, big-time. Z says the guy was playing off your desire for power—you know, your wanting to be somebody. He says that's pretty common, too."

"So all that King Louis stuff?"

"Counterfeit. The devil using Maxwell to con you."

"But what about—I mean, he said he believed in Jesus. He even prayed with us. How can you pray to God if you don't believe in him?"

Mom shook her head. "I've been thinking about that, honey. It could be Maxwell *was* praying, but to his god, not to the real God.

Or it could be he just knew the right things to say and do to make us believe in and trust him. Either way, he used just enough of what sounded like the truth to put us off guard."

"That's what makes this occult stuff so dangerous," Scotty added. "It's just close enough to the truth to fool people—especially those who want to be a somebody."

A sinking feeling began somewhere in Becka's chest and continued down into her stomach. Scott was right. She *had* wanted to be a somebody. A headline-maker. Unfortunately, the only headlines she would have made were in the obituary column. She took a deep breath. "Why would he choose me?"

"Maxwell?" he asked.

She nodded.

"The same reason he chose me," Mom answered. "Either he thought we were really something special, or . . ." Mom hesitated, unsure whether she should continue.

Scott saved her the trouble. "Or the Society was using him to hurt us."

Becka threw her brother a look.

Scott shrugged. "They're still pretty steamed about that little encounter with them and their Ouija board."

Becka took another deep breath and stared at the ceiling. Which was it? Was Maxwell deceived about her, or was he—she gave a little shudder—or was he trying to destroy her?

"Where is he now?" she asked. "Maxwell, I mean."

"San Francisco," Scott answered. "Some international 'cosmic gathering.'"

"I was so stupid," Becka groaned.

"No argument there," Scott agreed.

"Well, at least it's over," she sighed. But then she noticed Mom and Scott exchanging looks again. "What's wrong?" she asked. "It is over, isn't it?"

"Not entirely, dear," Mom answered.

There was a brief pause, which Scott broke. "Z thinks maybe we should, you know, pray. To make sure there isn't any left-over demonic junk." Becka looked at him. "I mean, you were into all that power and light stuff pretty deep," he added.

For a split second, Becka's temper flared, but the sincerity in Scott's and Mom's faces cooled it. Maybe they were right. After all, she had gotten pretty cozy with the whole "power" thing, and she had definitely experienced stuff that didn't come from her own imagination. "What . . ." Her voice was a little hoarse. "What am I supposed to do?"

"It's just like in Brazil," Mom offered. "Remember the Bible studies? When someone involved in witchcraft wanted to be a

Christian, remember how we had them renounce all the power they had experienced and ask Christ to replace it with his Spirit?"

Have I gone that far? Becka thought. She wasn't sure. And she knew her mother and brother weren't, either. Still, after all she'd been through, it definitely wouldn't hurt to play it safe.

She looked back at Mom, her admiration growing. She'd almost forgotten how much she loved and respected her mother.

She turned to Scott. He was doing his usual Cheshire cat grin. She loved him too. Though she'd never go out of her way to bring the subject to his attention.

"Well," she finally sighed, "I guess there's no time like the present. Shall we do it?"

A look of relief crossed Mom's and Scott's faces as they moved in a little closer. They each took one of Becka's hands, and Mom gave the hand she held a little kiss. Scott gave his a little squeeze. And then, right there in the hospital room, all three bowed their heads and started praying.

~

Later that night Scott chomped on a carrot as he entered his room and snapped on the light.

"*SQUAWK!* COWABUNGA, DUDE. COW-ABUNGA!"

"Hey, Cornelius," he said, unzipping his jacket and tossing it onto the bed. "We haven't talked much."

The bird bobbed his head up and down as if agreeing. "WHERE'S THE BEEF, WHERE'S THE BEEF, WHERE'S THE BEEF?"

Scott took another bite of carrot and slid into the chair behind his desk. "We're going to have to teach you some hipper sayings, old buddy."

The parrot leaped from his perch and fluttered down onto the desk. "WHERE'S THE BEEF, WHERE'S THE BEEF, WHERE'S THE BEEF?"

Scott held the carrot between his teeth and leaned forward. In a flash Cornelius reached over and snatched it from his mouth. The bird quickly waddled to the far end of the desk with his new prize. And balancing on one foot, he held up the carrot with the other and started nibbling away.

Scott glanced at his radio alarm: 9:04 P.M. Time to see if Z was on-line. He turned on the computer, dialed up the bulletin board, made a few clicks of the mouse, and typed:

Z? Are you there?

Good evening, New Kid.
I just got back from visiting Becky.

Before he could continue, Z answered:

I'm glad she finally regained consciousness.

This guy was unbelievable. Scott quickly
typed:

*Will you stop that? How do you know that sort of
stuff?!*

He waited for a reply, but there was none.
Finally words appeared on the screen. Once
again Z had changed the subject:

Did you enjoy your meeting with Nagaina?
*That was pretty sneaky—making us ride all the
way out to those houses, thinking we'd finally
meet you.*
Almost as sneaky as you trying to find out where I
live.

Scott raised an eyebrow. The man had a
point. But Z wasn't finished:

I thought Nagaina's experiences would be far
more beneficial to you than mine.
She sure made her point about reincarnation.

153

Funny, isn't it? On the surface it seems innocent enough. But when you follow reincarnation to its logical conclusion, you find bigotry, prejudice, indifference toward human pain, and most important, a direct conflict with Christ's purpose for dying on the cross.

Well, at least it's over.

Not entirely.

Scott felt a chill.

What do you mean?

There was a pause. The words formed . . . more slowly than before:

For some reason you have been singled out. I am afraid this was just another battle in what appears to be an ongoing war.

Somehow Scott had already guessed as much. He typed:

What's next?

I am not certain. However, I would look into that strange noise and light in your garage before too many more days pass.

Scott caught his breath. The noise. He'd

almost forgotten. But with that thought came another:

Who told you about the noise and light?
Z?
Z? Who told you about the noise?
Good night, New Kid.
No, hold it a minute.
Hold it!

He waited, continuing to stare at the screen. But there was no answer. Z had signed off.

"BEAM ME UP, SCOTTY, BEAM ME UP." Cornelius had trotted over to Scott's keyboard. Once again he was bobbing his head up and down for attention.

Scott reached out and scratched under the bird's neck as he continued staring at the screen, wondering.

They defeated the Society. . . .
   They overcame the dark power of
      the guru of lies. . . .
   Now they must face the Spell.
But Becka and Scott may not win this time,
   because they're fighting an enemy
   that is far more powerful than they realize.

FORBIDDEN DOORS #3
The Spell

BILL MYERS

The six robed figures stood in a secluded clearing of the park. It was surrounded by trees, and the overgrown bushes made it impossible to see from the road. This was good. This was exactly what they wanted.

As usual for this time of year, the fog had rolled in from the beach and blotted out all light from the moon and stars. This was good, too. Now there was only the glow of six candles—five black, one white—on the picnic table, the orange light flickering on the young faces.

There were two boys and four girls. Teenagers. Dressed in homemade robes with hoods. All had been drinking. And the red, watery eyes of the boys showed clear signs of smoking dope. Lots of it.

The rat had already been killed. Broken neck. Now the leader of those gathered, a chunky brunette with an obvious dye job, was carefully draining the animal's blood, filling the bottom half of a torn Diet Coke can with the dark liquid.

The boys snickered. It may have been from the booze or the dope or just from the chill of what they were doing. No one knew. But it was obvious they weren't taking the ceremony seriously.

Laura Henderson, a brooding blonde whose face was ravaged by acne, gave them a scowl. This was important business. After all, their leader had been humiliated—not once, but twice—by a family who had moved into their city barely a month ago. First there was the younger brother, a certain Scott Williams, who had dared challenge the leader's powers with the Ouija board. And he'd done it right in front of the entire Society. Then there was the older sister, Rebecca Williams. . . .

Henderson's eyes narrowed at the thought of the girl. Quiet, not really a standout in any sense. And yet she had been handpicked by the famous guru, Maxwell Taylor, for her "gifts." Laura scowled. How did such a nobody rate that kind of honor? As if that wasn't bad enough, the Williams crud had pulled a crazy stunt with a train—a stunt that, as far as Laura was concerned, proved she was trying to compete with the Society's leader for power.

Henderson could not have that. Their leader meant too much to her. She lived for the leader's praise; wilted at her criticism. *Power?* Henderson thought. *So be it. If this Williams girl wants power, we'll show her power.* She closed her eyes and began to recite: "Hate your enemies with your whole heart. . . ."

The other two girls joined in, and the chant grew louder, more concentrated: "And if a man smites you on the cheek, *smash* him on the other!"

The boys smirked and stifled a laugh. Henderson opened her eyes and cut them with an icy glare. After another snicker and a shrug of indifference, they also joined in.

"Hate your enemies with your whole

heart, and if a man smites you on the cheek, *smash* him on the other!

The leader set the rat carcass on the picnic table and reached into her robe, pulling out a feathered quill and a piece of homemade parchment.

The chant continued.

"Hate your enemies with your whole heart. . . ."

Laura dipped the quill into the can of blood.

"And if a man smites you on the cheek, *smash* him on the other!"

And then she wrote:

Rebecca

"Hate your enemies with your whole heart. . . ."

Williams

"And if a man smites you on the cheek, *smash* him on the other!"

Their voices grew louder. The booze, the drugs, the force of six people chanting together—it all gave them a kind of energy, a sense of belonging. Henderson drew a deep breath, her voice growing stronger, more determined, more . . . exhilarated.

162

The words of the chant echoed around her, filling the air, filling her head. This was the unity for which she hungered; the power she craved.

"Hate your enemies with your whole heart. . . ."

Laura set the pen down and raised the parchment above the flame of the white candle. The chanting grew more and more feverish. All eyes watched in eager anticipation.

"And if a man smites you on the cheek, smash *him on the other!"*

Suddenly the parchment ignited into a bright orange flame, the paper curling and crackling as it was consumed quickly and efficiently, until everything—including Becka's name—was nothing but ash.

The Forbidden Doors Series
The Society
The Deceived

Other Books by Bill Myers
Teen Books
Hot Topics, Tough Questions
*Christ B.C.: Becoming Closer Friends with the
    Hidden Christ of the Old Testament*

Youth Series
McGee and Me!
—*The Big Lie*
—*A Star in the Breaking*
—*The Not-So-Great Escape*
—*Skate Expectations*
—*Twister and Shout*
—*Back to the Drawing Board*
—*Do the Bright Thing*
—*Take Me Out of the Ballgame*
—*'Twas the Fight before Christmas*
—*In the Nick of Time*
—*Beauty in the Least*

The Incredible Worlds of Wally McDougle
—*My Life As a Smashed Burrito with Extra Hot
    Sauce*
—*My Life As Alien Monster Bait*
—*My Life As a Broken Bungee Cord*
—*My Life As Crocodile Junk Food*
—*My Life As Dinosaur Dental Floss*

—My Life As a Torpedo Test Target

Fantasy Series
Journeys to Fayrah
—The Portal
—The Experiment
—The Whirlwind
—The Tablet

If you liked the Forbidden Doors series...

...check out these additional Bill Myers titles!

MCGEE AND ME!

Meet Nick Martin, a normal kid with an unusual friend: the lively, animated McGee! All titles also available on video.